ENIGMA

LAUREL SPRINGS EMERGENCY RESPONSE
TEAM #3

LARAMIE BRISCOE

Editor: Elfwerks Editing

Beta Readers: Danielle Wentworth

Proofreader: Danielle Wentworth

Cover: Laramie Briscoe

Cover Photography: FuriousFotog

Formatting: Laramie Briscoe

ALSO BY LARAMIE BRISCOE

The Haldonia Monarchy

Royal Rebel

Royal Chaos

Royal Love

Heaven Hill Series

Meant To Be

Out of Darkness

Losing Control

Worth The Battle

Dirty Little Secret

Second Chance Love

Rough Patch

Beginning of Forever

Home Free

Shield My Heart

A Heaven Hill Christmas

Heaven Hill Next Generation

Hurricane

Wild

Fury

Heaven Hill Shorts

Caelin

Christine

Justice

Harley

Jagger

Charity

Liam

Drew

Dalton

Mandy

Rockin' Country Series

Only The Beginning

One Day at A Time

The Price of Love

Full Circle

Hard To Love

Reaper's Girl

The Nashvegas Trilogy

Power Couple

The Moonshine Task Force Series

Renegade

Tank

Havoc

Ace

Menace

Cruise

Laurel Springs Emergency Response Team

Ransom

Suppression

Enigma

Cutter

The MVP Duet

On the DL

MVP

The Midnight Cove Series

Inflame

Stand Alones

Sketch

Sass

Trick

Room 143

2018 Laramie Briscoe Compilation

2019 Laramie Briscoe Compilation

NEW RELEASE ALERTS

JOIN MY MAILING LIST

http://sitel.ink/LBList

JOIN MY READERS GROUP

fbl.ink/LaramiesLounge

MOONSHINE TASK FORCE MEMBERS

Ryan "Renegade" Kepler – Married to Whitney and father to Stella and Nick. Best friend to Trevor.

Trevor "Tank" Trumboldt – Married to Blaze, brother to Whitney, uncle to Stella and Nick. Best friend to Ryan.

Holden "Havoc" Thompson – Married to Leighton, father to Ransom and Cutter. Best friend to Mason.

Anthony "Ace" Bailey – Married to Violet.

Mason "Menace" Harrison – Married to Karina, father to Caleb and Kelsea, grandfather to Molly and Levi. Best friend to Holden.

Caleb "Cruise" Harrison – Married to Ruby, father to Molly and Levi, son of Mason, brother to Kelsea.

AUTHOR'S NOTE

I am aware of the inaccuracies in some of the legal scenes in the book. I'm definitely taking liberties, and I do know that. Please don't message me telling me these things. Just know that this is fiction, and should be read as such!

BLURB

It's not how we make mistakes, but how we correct them that defines us...

Karsyn Fallaway

Tucker didn't stop my car as it drove away from his house that summer night, and the sting of rejection hasn't gone away. Over a year has gone by, and I find myself looking for him in all the places he'd been before. It doesn't help, he's still an enigma I have yet to figure out.

My friends are the only thing holding me together. Work is the one thing keeping my mind busy.

Until my life threatens to tear completely apart.

Tucker Williams

She drove away and my pride wouldn't allow me to stop her. A year later, regret keeps me up at night, forcing me to replay the moment in my head. Working with the K-9's is the only thing keeping me going. Becoming close with the former MTF is a perk I hadn't counted on.

When a child is kidnapped, all the hard feelings have to be put aside to save a life.

Secrets are unearthed, and this time as Karsyn threatens to break, I know I'm the one to put her back together.

PROLOGUE

Karsyn

"THIS ISN'T WORKING FOR ME."

My heart drops as I hear the words coming out of Tucker's mouth. They aren't really computing with me though. He can't be saying what I think he's saying. "What?" I want to make sure I'm hearing him right.

"This." He motions between the two of us. "Isn't working for me."

I will not cry. I will not cry. I will not cry.

"You want more from me than I can give."

"Is this because I told you how I felt? Because I told you I love you?"

"Karsyn," he starts.

I hold up my hand. "Don't give me the it's not you, it's me bullshit." And cue the tears. They're falling now, huge and ugly. I'm not a cute crier. Not like those girls who refuse to let people see them break down. I've spent enough of my life holding things in, running from a past that would have broken most. I refuse to hold my feelings in. Our time on earth is finite, and I had to tell Tuck when I fell.

"It is." He reaches out for my hand, but I snatch it away. "I'm not the type of guy who gives into feelings. You have to understand where I came from."

"How can I, if you won't tell me?"

I cross my arms over my chest, looking at him, willing my bottom lip not to tremble. It does. No matter how hard I try to hold it still.

"I really am sorry, Syn."

"Sorry? Go to hell, Tuck."

"Already there, babe."

That line infuriates me. "Because you choose to be, and you don't get to call me *babe* anymore," I yell.

"You're right." He backs away, holding his hands up as if he's surrendering.

I can't take anymore. I grab my bag, tripping over Major as he comes to investigate what's going on. He barks, unsure of why I'm leaving.

"I gotta go, bud," I cry harder, scratching his head. I lean down, kissing him. "I love you, and I want you to keep him safe," I whisper.

He whines when I walk to the door. It's the whine that almost keeps me from walking out.

Almost.

But it's not enough.

I walk out with my head high, get in my car, and drive away. I can see them in the rearview, and in my mind, I beg him to stop me. He doesn't, and when I can no longer see them, I give into the tears. The gut-wrenching sobs and the absolute devastation of this chapter of my life coming to an end.

CHAPTER ONE

Tucker

WHEN DID I become the kind of guy who sits in a police car outside his ex-girlfriend's apartment? Especially when we didn't even put a label on it and it was never meant to be more than a couple of hook-ups.

My conscience blasts me for being the asshole I am. You became that guy when you decided to be a jerk and break it off with her because you couldn't handle the feelings she evoked in you. At this point I tell my conscience to shut the fuck up, even though it's completely right.

If I were anyone else, I'd tell them to get over it, stop going by her apartment and move on, but I can't. Not in a skeevy way either. There's nothing nefarious in the feelings I have for Karsyn.

I fucking miss her; I miss the way she made me feel, the way she took care of me, and the way she allowed me to be myself, even when the days were harder than I cared to admit. Behind me, my K-9 Major barks, letting me know I've been sitting here for too long.

"I hear ya, but just a few more minutes."

She's just pulled up in her sports car. The one I pulled her over in - it's how we met. I was used to girls being flirty with me; if they're cute, they're always flirty with a guy in uniform. But her? She was more than cute. Her hazel eyes haunted me - they weren't quite green, not quiet brown, something in between that I desperately wanted to know the answer to. She'd left her phone number on the ticket, but I hadn't had the guts to call her back. Not long after, I'd seen her at the grocery store and I'd asked her out.

She'd laughed and told me she didn't date cops who gave her tickets and I'd laughed telling her I didn't date women I'd given tickets, but here we are.

For months it went great. Nine to be exact. We were everything each other needed, until we weren't. There was no way to stop the downfall once it started. Once she told me her feelings and I didn't reciprocate, we were done for. I tried though, tried to tell her how important she was to me, how much I needed her to be a part of my life, and how much Major still looks for her. Every week I send her flowers.

Kels tells me she keeps them, including the cards that come with them, but I have yet to get a text message back, or any indication that she knows I've been following her, trying to get a glimpse of what our life together was like.

This is what I've been reduced to. Looking in from the very far outside, trying to figure out how to go on with my life without Karsyn Fallaway in it. It's been almost a year since the last time we talked, over a year and a half since we had anything resembling a relationship, and I'm beginning to think it's never going to happen. One day soon I'm going to have to swallow my pride and make a move. Forget all the shit we said to one another and just make it right. Because this right here? It's wrong.

I look down at my laptop, making a few notes about earlier incidents. Major starts barking. "Be quiet, bud, you'll give us away."

Looking up and over to where I know her car is, I see her. Her eyes looking right into mine. For the first time in over a year, she acknowledges me as she gives me a cautious wave. I wave back, grinning like a fool.

When she doesn't come toward me, but turns to go into her apartment, I know she doesn't want me to follow. She wants this to be it, she wants us to start slow, the way we should have before. My radio squawks, letting me know a K-9 has been requested and Ransom isn't available to take the call.

"Gotcha dispatch, Major and I are responding."

I give her one more glance, and as I drive away, I do it with a little sliver of hope, that what I thought was over maybe isn't. Just maybe, it isn't.

CHAPTER TWO

Karsyn

"HE WAS OUTSIDE MY APARTMENT AGAIN," I sigh to Kels as we sit outside the office, on our lunch break.

It's a seriously gorgeous spring day. One of the first ones we've had so far this year. Bitter coldness swept through Alabama this winter, and while the cold temperatures are long gone, ice still encompasses the vestiges of my heart. In more ways than one it was the coldest winter in my lifetime.

"When are you going to go over and talk to him? How long will you let him troll around like a creeper?" She giggles as she takes a drink of her decaf. When she was pregnant, she started drinking decaf and never went back once Ella was born.

I shrug. "It's kind of flattering."

"Imagine how emasculating it is for him though," she points out. "He's trying."

"He should try," I insist. "He broke my heart and stepped on it with his combat boot."

"But look at me." She takes a bite of her wrap. "I'm here, living the dream, even though you warned me to be careful with Nick."

Jealous doesn't even begin to describe how I feel about her relationship with Nick. I try to hold it back, because she absolutely deserves to be happy and to have the life she does. I just want my happily ever after too.

"Sometimes, holding on to the thing that hurts you, ends up keeping you from a happiness you only could have dreamed of." Her voice is soft, pointing out that I'm being stupid, like the mother she is.

Stabbing the piece of lettuce in my bowl, I nod. "I know, trust me I do. The flowers, every week without fail, show me how sorry he is."

We're quiet for a few minutes. "What exactly happened between the two of you?"

I haven't told anyone, because it's embarrassing, and it broke me.

"You don't have to tell me if you don't want to."

The truth is, I need to tell someone. If there's one thing I've learned in all the therapy I've been involved in, it's that I need to speak my truth. "No." I take a drink of my water. "I need to."

"You don't have to tell me just because I asked." She knocks my knee with hers.

"I know."

It takes me a few minutes to pull my thoughts together, along with a few bites of my salad. Nervously, I take another drink of water before I start. "Tucker and I met in a funny way. He gave me a speeding ticket, and I hit on him."

"Did you really?" She laughs, shaking her head.

"Yeah," I admit, a grin spreading across my face. "I'd

never been pulled over before, and I knew I was speeding. I was running late that day, and I was so worried I'd be fired, because I'd made some other stupid mistakes. It was right after I started this job, and I didn't want to be late."

Remembering how nervous I was back then, that I would be fired seems funny now. Since Stella quit we haven't found a good replacement, so basically Kels and I run this show. Most of the time we do a good job, but every once in a while, we find ourselves extremely fucked and have to call for back up.

"Anyway, he pulled me over, when I saw him, oh my god! He was so hot looking, and he walked up to the side of my car like he owned the damn thing."

"I'm well aware of that walk," Kels laughs, winking at me. "Nick has it down too."

"I watched him in my mirror, wondering who the hell he was, and what I could do to see him again."

"Could always break another law," she offers, a snort on the end of her suggestion.

Right now it sounds like a good idea, and I just might do it. Maybe it would break the ice to this situation we've found ourselves in.

"When he had me sign the ticket, I put my phone number on there."

She spits out her coffee. "You didn't!"

Giggling, I nod. "I did. He didn't call me."

"What an ass!"

"Right?" I agree with her, putting the lid on what's left of my salad. Somehow eating doesn't interest me, not while I'm telling her the story of how I met Tucker. "So a few weeks go by, I pay the ticket, like a good citizen. I'm in the park, running, training for that fucking couch to 5k I did, remember that?"

"We all did it and hated it, as an office."

"Yes! Back then I wasn't super close with you and Stella, so I didn't tell you everything."

She rolls her eyes. "You know you could have always told us anything."

"But I'm younger than you, and I thought you'd make fun of me."

No matter how they'd worked to make me a part of their group, being younger always made me feel at a disadvantage. From the day I met them in class, they've never treated me differently, but I see myself differently than I see them. Probably because they're older, and I always feel at a disadvantage. It's entirely on me, but the feeling is there.

"We wouldn't have. Look at who the two of us have ended up with."

Knowing what we know now, it does seem stupid, but back then it was a big deal for me. "Anyway, I was practicing in the park, I tripped over a break in the asphalt on the trail, and while I was sitting there, crying about how my pride was ruined and how bad it hurt, here comes Tucker."

"Like a fucking knight in shining armor." Kels grins.

God, I hate her sometimes, how she turns everything into a romance novel. "More like an annoyed dude with a dog." I roll my eyes.

"Sounds like Tucker."

"Exactly like Tucker. Being who he is, he took charge, carrying me the final mile back to our cars. I tried telling him I'm a medical assistant and could tell that I hadn't done major damage, but it was definitely a sprain. He wouldn't take no for an answer, he drove me to the twenty-four-hour clinic, and stayed with me while I called my parents."

The memories of that day wash over me with a fondness I miss. Everything was so easy then - feelings didn't get in the way.

"Then what happened? We've only got fifteen more minutes," Kels presses.

"A few weeks later, I saw him at the grocery store. On a whim I invited him for dinner, to thank him for what he did."

"Thanks for dinner." Tucker stretches. "You really didn't have to."

I've walked him out to his truck, and I'm not wanting the night to end, but he hasn't really given me any indication he'd like it to go further.

"You didn't have to help me down the rest of the trail, but you did."

He laughs, the sound a deep reverberation in his chest. "Trust me, it wasn't that hard. Carrying a woman like you against me for more than a mile? Don't even sweat it."

There may never be another chance for me to ask, so I'm going to take a shot. "Why didn't you ever call me?"

He blushes. He fucking blushes.

"Lots of women hit on me in my line of work," he starts. "I mean you're young and cute, I thought you were just trying to get out of a ticket."

I move closer to him, grabbing hold of the material of his shirt with my fingers. "And what about this? Do you think I'm just trying to thank you for helping me?"

"The truth?"

"Always, Tucker. I'm not the kind of girl who wants to hear things that are just supposed to make me happy."

"At first, yeah I thought you were being nice, but I'm feeling something."

Great, because I am too. "It's not just you."

Knowing this may be my only chance, I lift up on my tiptoes, crushing my lips against his. He's taller than me by a lot. His strong arms go around me, lifting me against him, so that I'm even with his lips. Stronger than I ever imagine a man could be, he turns me around, wrestles the door of his truck open, and manages to sit me on the leather seat.

"It's not just me," he gasps, pushing my hair back from my face. "There's something here, isn't there?"

"Yeah." I curl my hands around his shoulders, going in for another taste of him.

My whole life I've had boys, but him? He's an actual man.

"After that, the two of us started hanging out, hooking up, and we kept telling each other it was just for fun."

"But it wasn't, was it?" Kels whispers.

I whisper back, wishing the tears wouldn't build in my eyes the way they are now. "It started out that way." I shrug. "I tried to keep my feelings out of it, because he was truthful with what he wanted, but I caught feelings."

"Did you tell him?"

My biggest regret. "Yeah, and when I did, it was over."

She puts her hand on my shoulder. "Over?"

"Yeah, it was like he successfully erased me from his life."

"I guarantee you, he didn't," she argues.

But I know. "It felt like it. One day we were together every day, and then it was like he flipped a switch and didn't even know me anymore."

"He's trying now, though," Kels reminds me.

"The question is, will I open myself up to him again?"

She gets up, grabbing our stuff to throw it away. Our lunch break is over and we have to get back to work.

"Only you know what you can deal with, Karsyn."

And that's the million-dollar question, because I know without a doubt, I'd deal with a lot just to feel his arms wrap around me again.

CHAPTER THREE

Tucker

"YOU'RE SLIPPIN'." Nick gives me a grin as he comes into the conference room at the biggest hotel we have in our small town.

It's time for a meeting of the Laurel Springs Emergency Response Team, and any of us who can attend have convened here. "What do you mean, I'm slippin'?"

He chuckles. "Heard through the grapevine you only sent one rose to Karsyn this week."

The grapevine means Kels, and I did only send one rose. "Fuck you, she knows what it means."

"Does she?" He nods to the door, where she's walking in beside one of the new EMT's working with Cutter. I don't know the asshole's name, but she's smiling and he's grinning.

They laugh at something, and it's like a damn knife through my heart. She doesn't even look at me as she takes a seat next to Stella. Major, sitting at my feet, sniffs as he smells Karsyn and looks up at me. "Go on." I give him a gentle nudge.

Just because she's blocking me out doesn't mean she'll block him out. For that I'm grateful, because he totally loves her. Almost as much as I do.

She makes a sound of excitement as he hops up in her lap, licking at her chin. "Hey, buddy." She gives him praise. "Haven't seen you in a while."

It's been eleven months and twenty-nine days since we had a conversation. Not that I'm keeping track or anything, but it's been eleven months since she gave me my shit, and I turned my back on her. She gave me a shot that day, promising she would help me through whatever it was holding me back. I didn't believe her and did what I always do - count on myself. Worst mistake of my life, and I keep promising I'm going to change it, but I don't want to ruin what little respect she still has for me. There's a part of me that wants to go over, have a seat next to her, and reclaim my spot in her life. But that's selfish and a total dick move.

"She loves the dog more than you." Nick elbows me.

"I hate you," I growl. "Fucking hate you."

"Because I'm married, and have everything you want?" he taunts.

Yes. That's exactly it. But I can't bring myself to admit it to him. Admitting it to him would mean admitting it to myself, and I just can't do it yet. "Because you're annoying as hell. When did you start smiling all the damn time, anyway?"

"Got married and got everything I want." He winks.

Fucking hate him.

That's when I look across the room to my dog. The one who is supposed to be my partner, the one who has my back no matter what? He's got his head in Karsyn's lap, looking up at her like he's lovesick. When I snap my fingers, he turns to me, but doesn't move. He gives me a half-hearted look, whining slightly before he turns his head back into her lap, eating up the head scratches she's giving him. I don't let my eyes travel to hers. If we lock eyes, it's over. She'll see it all, because I'm sick of hiding it.

Major hops down, curling at her feet. Even my dog has abandoned ship.

Fuck my life. This sucks.

"OFFICER WILLIAMS, please come forward and tell us about what you do with the Laurel Springs Police Department."

I sigh silently. This councilwoman has hit on me every single time we've been around one another. I've tried to dissuade her, but she keeps it up. As I get up and step toward her, she gives me a private smile. It's one I don't want and I refuse to give back to her.

As I take my place at the front, I give a little wave to the members of the LSERT present today. "Hey, I'm Tucker Williams, and I'm the K-9 trainer for the greater northern Alabama area, as well as being a K-9 officer." I clear my throat, letting my gaze fall onto Karsyn.

She's pretending not to listen, but I can see the pride on her face, even though she keeps it turned away from me. I click my tongue and Major comes to my side. "Heel." I point down to the ground. He sits next to me, patiently waiting his next command, calmly looking over the crowd.

"Right now there are a total of four K-9's for our half of the state. Major is new to me; we've been together for two years, Ransom has Rambo who has been a defining piece of this puzzle to get us more dogs, and then Birmingham has two K-9's. For the most part Ransom and I deal with everything north of Birmingham. What we want to do is get enough funds to purchase two more dogs, but that runs around twenty thousand dollars." I look down at Major, petting him.

"How would you raise this money?" the EMT who walked in with Karsyn asks.

"Good question, that's what I'm talking to you all for. Bottom line is we need the dogs. Rambo alone has proven his worth, if we had two more like him?"

"There's no other dog like Rambo," Stella says loud enough for everyone to hear.

There are giggles around the room, and I can't help but laugh too. "Touché. But I think y'all understand what I'm getting at. These dogs are another line of defense against a number of threats to our town. They track missing people, wanted people, they smell dope, and just like you all saw Rambo do, they can go after one perpetrator while we go after another. They are expensive, but they will more than prove their worth."

I'm losing the room, I can tell. The EMT opens his mouth again. "I suppose you will train them?"

"Affirmative."

"Who takes your spot while you're training them?"

This time I don't have to answer the question. Karsyn does it for me. She's well aware of my schedule.

"He works overtime to make sure the people in this part of the state are well taken care of. He trained dogs in the military and there's no one more equipped to handle one like he is. If Tucker says we need two dogs, then I firmly believe we need two dogs."

Our eyes meet for the first time in longer than I care to admit. She's not smiling at me, but she's silently giving me the strength I need to proceed. Public speaking isn't my strong suit, but I'm here in the interest of the community.

"As Ms. Fallaway said, I'll work overtime to make sure the dogs are properly trained. Dogs can learn a lot from one another too, so one of the best things will be them all getting a chance to be together. I've done research and there's one dog available in the next few weeks. We, as an organization, can apply for a government stipend, or we can raise the money on our own."

"Again," the fucker interrupts me, "where are we going to get even ten thousand dollars, much less twenty?"

I've about had it with him. "Where do the kids get their money for what they want?"

Stella's eyes brighten. She's with me and shows as much as she begins to speak. If there's one thing Stella loves, it's dogs, and I know she's sick of Ransom working all-nighters when he's needed. With their baby, I know she wants him home more often than not. "They do bake sales, car washes, ask for donations."

"Exactly." I nod. "I know it's not going to be easy, but with some elbow grease and a lot of hard work, we can get what we need, and if we're serious about this, then that's what we'll have to do."

Nick speaks up from where he sits. "I can guarantee D will help with this. If we ask the kids of the community for their help, they'll help. We just have to put it out there."

"Okay." The councilwoman stands next to me, putting

her hand along my waist. I do my best to slink away, but she's determined. "Who will be heading this thing up?" she asks.

"I can help." Karsyn raises her hand. "I know a thing or two about fundraisers. I was a cheerleader in high school."

The EMT gives me a smartass smile. "Seems to me since this is something Officer Williams wants, he should be the one to head it up. I mean, only seems fair."

Work with Karsyn? I'll take it. I give him a huge smile. "Ya know? You're right, I would love to help Ms. Fallaway head this up. I am the one requesting the extra manpower."

"It's settled then," the councilwoman says. "When we meet next week, hopefully the two of you will have some ideas for what we can do."

The meeting breaks up after this, and I notice Karsyn isn't getting up to leave. Looks like the two of us are about to speak the first words we've spoken to one another in too long a time.

"Thanks for offering to help." My voice is soft as I approach her. She looks up, her gaze meeting me straight on. I love those eyes of hers, so fucking expressive, especially when I've done something she likes.

"It wasn't for you, Tucker. You and I both know Laurel Springs needs these improvements. It'll help everyone."

But I see it, in her eyes. She wants to be here with me, just like I want to be with her. As soon as we quit lying to ourselves, the better off we'll be.

The only question is, who will give in first?

CHAPTER FOUR

Karsyn

I SHIFT in the booth at The Café, waiting for Tucker to get here. After the LSERT meeting, we'd quickly decided to meet in public for our first brainstorming session. I don't know if that was more for me than him. In our previous attempt at a relationship, we'd never gone out in public together. Not because we hadn't wanted to, but because we couldn't keep our hands off each other.

More than once he'd come to pick me up for dinner, and we'd ended up in bed.

This is going to be a test of epic proportions. Checking my phone, I see he's got a few more minutes to get here. I was earlier than I'd expected to be.

"Do you want anything while you wait?" Leigh asks as she walks by the booth.

"Ya know what? I'll take an order of fries and a Coke."

Fries are my go-to, I'll eat them any day of the week, any way they come.

"Anything else?"

Immediately I think about who's meeting me. "An order of cheese sticks along with a Sprite, some water and a treat for Major?"

She grins. "Will do, I'll have it all out to ya in a few minutes."

"Take your time."

My gaze travels along the parking section in front of the building, this time zeroing in on a Laurel Springs PD SUV. It's Tucker. I can see him, opening the back door of the driver's side to let Major out. The two of them make an imposing team as they walk toward the entrance. Major is a big boy, standing to about Tucker's knees, and Tucker? He's a man in charge. He walks everywhere like he owns the damn place.

He holds the door open for a woman carrying a baby, and my stomach cramps. At one point, I'd thought maybe the two of us would have that in the future. Then I told him how I felt, and it was over.

They walk over to where I'm sitting. His eyes move to the spot beside me, before he takes the spot across from me. Major takes a spot underneath the booth at our feet.

"Surprised you're sitting with your back to the door," I comment, as I situate myself so that my feet aren't in Major's way.

"Didn't think you'd be okay with me sitting all up next to you," he answers, rubbing a hand over his facial hair.

Truthfully, I probably wouldn't have minded it. Instead, I poke the bear. "Good, didn't want you over here anyway."

A slow grin slides across his face. "Yeah, okay."

Leigh picks that moment to bring the food and drinks, reaching under the table, she gives Major his stuff, petting him on the head. "I heard you two have major planning to do, so I'll leave you alone. If you need anything, please let me know!"

I've brought a notebook and a pouch of pens with me. So many people prefer to use their laptops or phones to keep track of their to-do lists, or their day-to-day activities. Not me, there's something so satisfying about making lists in different colors of pen, and then marking the tasks off as I go. Grabbing them out of my bag, I put them on the table in front of me, next to my fries.

"You ordered for me?" he asks with a raised eyebrow.

"I hope you haven't changed your tastes that much. I mean I used to know what you liked." I shift uneasily in my seat. Maybe he's changed and I just didn't know it.

"The things I've changed haven't been my taste, Syn, not at all."

I shiver as I hear the nickname he gave me on his lips. He'd joked once that even though he'd sinned a lot, I was his favorite. Then he'd written it on one of the first flowers he'd sent me, and the way he spelled it, had warmed my heart too. Why the spelling of a name got to me, I'll never know. Maybe it's because it was specific to the way my parents spelled mine.

"Good." I do my best not to meet his chocolate brown eyes. Those things – I could get lost in, and then we'd be fucked for this meeting.

He breaks our gaze, reaching over to grab the seasoned salt on the tables here. He shakes it generously over my plate, knowing intimate details of my preferences. Then he grabs the bottle of ketchup, putting a dollop on the side of my plate. I'm a dipper, and he damn well knows it.

"Thank you," I whisper.

"My pleasure."

The way he says those words is a tease in and of itself. We knew so much pleasure together, more pleasure than I've ever known with anyone else. His fingers and tongue could pull sounds from me like no other. I miss it, miss the way he'd hold me tight to him as he plunged into my body, miss the way he kissed my forehead when we were done. Pulling my notebook closer to me, I clear my throat.

"So about that brainstorming?"

There's a lull in our conversation as our gazes go separate ways, and we both take a bite of our respective food. The way he eats is even a turn on; most men go right for it, shoving food in their mouth. Not Tucker. He takes polite bites, chews until he's done, then swallows, licking his lips to get the remaining crumbs off them, before he speaks.

"Nick seemed to think D would have some good ideas, I definitely think we should get him involved."

"Me too." I'm excited to work with the youth of the community. I missed out on a lot of this growing up the way I did.

"What about a car wash? A bake sale? We could all get together and have sign ups. We could take different shifts. People could pay to have their pictures taken with Rambo."

"Oh that's a good idea," he laughs. "People love Rambo."

"You guys could pose for a calendar." I give him a sly grin. "I'm sure we'd make a ton of money that way."

"You saying I'm hot?"

I roll my eyes as I take another bite of my fries. "You know you're hot, you don't need me to tell you that. All of you are hot. What do you think?"

He rubs his beard. "Let me talk to the guys about it. Their wives might have something to say."

"Then you could do a bachelor calendar with the members of the LSERT," I suggest.

His gaze is serious as it meets mine. "You and I both know I'm not a bachelor."

My heart pounds. "Aren't you? Isn't that what you said you're going to be the rest of your life?"

There's a ticking in his jaw and I know I've hit a nerve. Something forces me to keep going, even though I know it's not in our best interests.

"Things change, Karsyn." His teeth grind together. "Sometimes you don't know yourself as well as you thought you did."

I can't help it. Fuck it still hurts the way he threw my feelings away. "Or maybe you're just confusing lust and fucking with a real relationship. I mean, you wouldn't be the first, would you, Tuck?"

He's pissed now, I can see it in the way he's holding his body tight, the way his eyes are darting around the room, looking anywhere but at me. "No, I wouldn't, and I'm sorry about that."

"Mmm hmmm." My tone is dismissive.

"When are you going to believe me?" he whispers, reaching for my hand. "What do I have to do to get you to give me another chance?"

For so long I thought declarations of love would be the way to get to my heart, but he's made those in the flowers he sends every week. What he doesn't get is I'm a lover of the little things, and maybe it's time I tell him.

"You want to know what I'm looking for, Tuck?"

"Please." The word is ripped from his throat, hoarse and emotive, a dying man begging for a drink of water.

"The shit that matters. I love the flowers every week, but

the one flower? It means more, and you know why. Stopping by because you can't stand not to see me, notes on my car, a just thinking of you text, being there for me when I have a bad day." I furiously wipe away tears, pissed that they're falling and really irritated that my voice is choked when the next words press against my lips. "And making me feel safe," I sob uncontrollably, with the effort of trying to keep it together. "Because you." I point to him. "You know I never feel safe. But with you." I push again at the moisture under my eyes. "I always, always felt safe."

"Syn." His voice is tight now as he reaches for my hand.

I can't do it though, I've laid too much on the line here tonight, I've opened myself up too wide to sit here a minute longer. Even though Major is noticing my distress and is pawing at my feet. "Not right now." I gather up my stuff, scooting out of the booth. "Please, let me leave here with some dignity."

He nods, his own eyes showing moisture behind the lids. Maybe I'm not the only one heartbroken here. "I'll make sure you get home safe."

"You always do," I whisper, because I know he follows me. "You always do."

CHAPTER FIVE

Tucker

I DON'T DO WELL with days off, not anymore. They used to be filled doing mundane shit with Karsyn – her teaching me how to bake a cake, going with her to pick out a dress for a work event she had to attend, helping her wash her car. Back then I didn't realize how much I looked forward to the mundane shit. I believe I even grumbled a time or two. Funny how you don't miss what you had until it's gone.

Today I would love to bake a cake with her, help her wash her car, just have her here. The loneliness is the worst. Some days it eats at me, other days I don't mind it much, today it threatens to drive me out of my fucking mind.

Major lays on the couch with me, his head resting on my thigh. He looks up at me, a little whine escaping. He misses her too, the hole her being gone has left in our lives is big. I'm not sure I can take my company anymore, and I'm almost sure he's sick of me too.

"I know, we need to go and do something."

Even in the middle of my pity party, I know it's not helping anyone, especially me. I've laid around too long and thought life would fix itself without me doing much to change it. Today I realize I have to change it, and I have to do something to make that change happen. No more sitting around hoping for a difference. Starting today I'm going to work for it.

"Let's go." I tap my thigh.

I have an idea, but I don't know how well it'll be received. I'm thinking about what Karsyn said when we saw each other last. We hop in my truck and I head to town, to a store I've never been to.

XOXO opened not long ago. I heard about it from Ransom. Apparently Leigh has a thing for pens, and this place has the biggest selection in Alabama, at least that's what he said. Ransom tends to exaggerate, but who am I to say until I go in? I park in the nearest spot, checking to make sure it's open. "You wanna come or stay?" I ask Major.

He hops over me, out of the truck before I am. "Guess I know what that means," I laugh, shaking my head.

Together, the two of us enter as quietly as we can. But Major isn't great about being quiet; his tags jingly loudly, along with a bell over the door. It announces our presence so loudly we could be standing before a king.

"Be there in a second," a voice yells from the back.

"Take your time."

Getting my first good look at the place, I'm overwhelmed. Paper, pens, all things cutesy are everywhere. Pink, purple, that rosy gold color that Karsyn loves - it all looks like it threw up in here, along with a container of glitter. Good Lord, I've stumbled into my version of hell, and Karsyn's version of heaven.

"You look scared," a woman just a little taller than my collarbone laughs as she sees my face. "And so does he."

Looking down, I see Major on the ground, his paws over his eyes. We're horrified.

"We're not used to so much femininity." I do my best to defend our positions.

She giggles, not offended at all. "What can I help you with?"

I rub at the beard on my face, a gesture I've picked up recently. It's a nervous tell, one I'm gonna have to get rid of. "There's this woman," I start.

"Isn't there always?"

"Oh my God, yes," I chuckle. "But anyway, there's this woman I'm trying to get on the good side of. She's a planner."

"She make her own, or does she buy premade?" She interrupts, her gaze already darting back and forth between the front and back of her store.

"She makes her own. The amount of pens and paper she has is amazing. She has these little tapes too; they are different, but she always bitched about not being able to get her lines straight." Telling her this makes me remember back to the nights we sat together. It was my favorite time. I'd be working on plans to train the next week, and she'd be making her to-do lists for what she wanted to accomplish. I miss those moments, more than I should be allowed to.

"I have the perfect thing for you." She immediately starts walking to the back. "We got this new set of rulers and measuring tools earlier this week. I've tried them out, and they are the best," she says as she puts them in my hands.

"If you say so, I will believe you."

"What else does she like?"

"Pens. Outline pens, felt tip, double-sided. Anything like

that, but do you have something new? Chances are she's already got it if it's older."

She smiles brightly. "I have some in the back, actually. These are brand-new. They make their own outline. They're awesome."

"I'll take them."

"Perfect." She goes to the back, getting what she's described to me.

Major looks at me, his gaze just on this side of disapproving. "We want Karsyn back, don't we?" I grumble at him. He makes a noise, and I know he understands what I'm saying.

When she brings everything up, she looks at me, questions in her eyes. "I heard you say the name Karsyn to your dog. Is it the Karsyn that works at Dr. Patterson's?"

"That's her."

"She comes in a lot, she's actually been asking about these pens." She grins. "I've been expecting them for a few weeks. They were on backorder."

"Is there anything else she eyes when she comes in here, ya know that she won't buy herself?"

This woman is an asset, and I would be stupid not to use her as such.

"That tote over there." She points to a tote that reads *Totes y'all*. "It's from an actresses' line, and it's expensive."

With the information she's given me, I walk over, don't even look at the price tag, and throw it on the counter. "I'll take it too."

"Do you want me to make this pretty for you? Like a gift?" She raises an eyebrow. "I get the feeling this is definitely a gift."

"Work your magic."

The price I pay for everything is in the three figures, but

I don't even care. I would give all my time, spend all my money to have Karsyn back again. Whatever it takes to prove to her that I do pay attention, I do love her, and I do want her in my life.

When I leave the store thirty minutes later, I'm holding the bag with all the goodies in it. "Okay, let's go get our other part of the gift." I open the door, putting the bag in the truck. Major looks like he wants to jump up. "Leave it." I tell him sternly, letting him know I want him to stay beside me.

"Okay." I tap my thigh when I close the door. Together we head for the bakery. When I walk in, my stomach growls, reminding me I haven't eaten today.

"What ya gonna get today, officer?"

I peruse what's in the case. I can never remember the girl behind the counter's name, but she always gives us discounts and she's pleasant to speak with. "How about one of those pimento cheese sandwiches to go, and can I get two of the red velvet cupcakes in a to-go container?"

"Sure, you want something for Major too?" She eyes him, making kissy faces at him. They like each other a lot.

"I guess so." I roll my eyes in a good-natured way.

"Come on," she tells him with an excitement in her voice. He immediately goes behind the counter, and she gives him a treat she keeps back there for the K-9's. They love this place almost as much as we do.

He gives her licks on the face, before he sits down patiently and waits for her to give him his treat.

"He's nicer for you than he is for me," I grumble.

"Because I don't make him work for it," she giggles. "Just a sec and I'll have your stuff ready for you."

In my mind, I'm trying to figure out how I'm going to play this. I don't think I want to take it inside to her office. I'd much prefer to put it in her car and let her find it. No matter how many times I told her too, she's never locked her doors and I have no doubt that's not changed.

When our order is done, we pay and then head back to the truck. Major sits on the floor, chewing on his treat, and I grip my shaking hands on the steering wheel. I literally have stared down guns and not been this nervous before. There's a part of me that wants to explore why that is. There's another part that tells me to shut up and just deal.

Her car is parked off to the side at Dr. Patterson's office, no one parked beside it. I pull in, going to her passenger side door, and sure enough it's unlocked. Quickly I put everything in I've purchased, pull out a clean piece of paper, and write a quick note. It's not a declaration of everything she means to me, but hopefully it lets her know I'm taking this seriously.

Almost as quick as we pulled in, we're gone, and I'm waiting with butterflies in my stomach for her to find my offering. I just hope she loves it as much as I love her.

CHAPTER SIX

Karsyn

IT'S BEEN A LONG DAY, and I can't help but be glad we're finally heading home. "See ya tomorrow." I wave to Kels. "Give those boys of yours a hug for me!"

She grins saucily. "I'm giving the oldest one a huge hug."

I roll my eyes, a smirk on my face as I look at her. I'm happy she's happy, but at the same time I'm slightly envious. "You know I mean the children."

"Totes my bad." She gets into her SUV, waving back at me.

Opening my car, I gratefully sink into the driver seat, glad to be off my feet. When I go to throw my lunchbox and purse into the passenger seat, I see something sitting there. My heart pounds up in my throat as I see a tote bag from XOXO I've been eyeing for months there, along with the signature packaging of the owner, Tori. I've been spending enough time in there lately I would notice it anywhere.

My hand shakes as I reach for the card attached to the

tote bag. I don't want to get my hopes up, but it's almost like telling a man dying of thirst not to walk to water. When I set it in front of me, on my steering wheel, I spy the manly scrawl I see at least once a week. But for some reason, the simple Syn, on this envelope brings tears to my eyes.

Syn,

I thought about what you said. A lot, and I think I realize what you're saying. I didn't return your declaration back then not because I didn't love you. I do love you, Karsyn. I love you so much I've been afraid to make myself vulnerable for you.

I know this sounds like a goddamn cliché. It's not you, it's me.

You have to understand the household I grew up in. Before I went into the military, I was a military kid. Nineteen moves over my childhood. I was always the new kid in town, and it was easier for me not to make friends and get hurt when I had to leave than to cry as our car pulled away leaving the people who I spent all my time with.

Dad was a hard military guy, and before he had his heart attack two years ago, he never told my mom he loved her in my presence.

I can learn, like Rambo and Major. I can learn, but babe, I need you to teach me. It was the biggest mistake of my life, to let you leave. Please, let me fix that mistake. Let me correct it.

We could be happy together - I believe that with all of my heart.

If you need more time, I understand. I can't undo the damage I've done with one tote bag, which I don't really get the significance of, or a few pens you like.

What I can do is wait, and Syn, I'll be here.

Doesn't matter when or where, I'll be here. Ready, when you're willing.

I love you.

Not so hard to write down on a piece of paper, but I swear to you, I'll get the words out in person if you let me.

I love you.

P.S. – Lock your damn door!

Tucker

Tears stream down my face, making it hard to read the lines after the first *I love you*. Who is this man? This isn't the Tucker I had a relationship with last year. If he had been open like this before, I wouldn't have left. I'd have refused to drive away, and I would have known we had something to fight for.

Going through the tote bag, I see the pens I've been waiting weeks on, the cupcakes I like from the bakery, and a couple of other things that are my favorites. All those times when I talked and I felt like he wasn't listening – he was.

I realize that part is my fault. I discounted the way he showed me he loved me. He always wanted me to text him when I got home. He'd growl about parking under a light at night, be super pissed that I don't lock my car doors at work, and he'd all the time wanted to take me to the gun range.

But me? I have secrets too. A big one I didn't want to share back then, and I think maybe it's time I come clean with him the same way he's come clean with me. Mine is bigger than his, and I know it needs to happen in person. I also know I'm not in the correct frame of mind just yet to tell him. I've never told anyone about what happened to me. Only my parents and the people of the town I grew up in know. When I came to Laurel Springs, I pushed all that behind me. It's only fair, if I want him to be completely honest with me, that I be completely honest with him.

With shaking hands, I grab one of my new pieces of stationary from the haul he got me, along with a pen.

Tuck,

I don't even know what to say. This gift is so amazing, and I promise you'll understand the significance of the tote bag.

What you wrote is more than I thought I would ever get from you. I thank you so much for being willing to share this much of yourself with me. I want to share this much of myself with you, but I'm not ready yet.

Just a little more time, Tuck, I promise. While there are things you haven't told me, there are things I haven't told you. If we go into this, this time, it needs to be with all our secrets laid bare. You laid them down for me, and I need to lay them down for you.

I won't keep you waiting the way I've kept you waiting for the past year. I promise.

I hope to see you in a few weeks.

I love you too, more than I've ever loved anyone.

P.S. – I never lock it because I'm in a hurry not to be out in the open. I'm always focused on getting wherever it is I need to be and shutting myself away. Maybe you could help me with feeling safer?

Love,

Karsyn

Immediately I start my car, putting it in drive to go the couple of miles across town. His house looks just like I remember it. Manly and well-maintained. He has room for a family, unlike my apartment. Major always hated being in my apartment, because there was nowhere for him to run.

Before I lose my nerve, I quickly get out, running to the front door. I put the envelope with my letter in the mail slot.

I always made fun of him for having a mail slot, but it was a piece of nostalgia he never wanted to get rid of.

Going back to my car, I leave before he can open the door and stop me. If he stops me this time, I won't be able to leave, and chances are we'll end up back in the exact same spot we're in now.

Tucker

I watch her. Through my *Ring* doorbell, but I don't stop her as she runs away. There are too many things up in the air for me to stop her. I made the first move by writing her a letter, now it's fair that I give her a chance to make the next move with a letter. I need to read the letter she put through my mail slot. Maybe I need to manage my expectations. What if she refuses to give me another chance? What if it's a flat-out no? Major barks as he hears her car leave, almost as if he's the one saying don't go.

Fuck, I rub my sternum with the heel of my hand. There's an actual pain there, one I'm not used to. Maybe it's heart burn and not the feeling of losing everything important to me. That's gonna hurt, but it's kinda what I deserve. Major is down on all fours, sniffing the envelope, nosing it toward me. I think he wants to me to open it as badly as I want to.

"Okay, okay. You're a demanding little shit sometimes."

My throat goes to my stomach as I start reading it, sure as hell she's going to tell me to fuck off. But I read her words slowly, let them sink in, digest them with the maturity I've gained over the past year.

I do something the old Tucker wouldn't have been comfortable with. I put the envelope on the table next to my bed, where I can see it every day, and I vow to wait. However long it takes, I'll wait for her to come to me. I won't pressure, I won't beg for an answer. I'll be the supportive man I should've been in the beginning. I'll show her the person I can be, and I promise to prove to her I'm worth the wait.

Major gets up on the bed, looking at me. It's like he's asking me where Karsyn is, almost like he expected her to be here since she was out on the porch. I run my hand over his head, giving him a scratch. The movement calms him and me at the same time.

"She's not ready yet, Bud. And that's okay. We'll be right here when she is."

He barks in what appears to be agreement.

Tonight when I go to sleep, it's with a smile on my face and a lightness in my heart. Things aren't perfect, but they're on the road to being what I want them to be. For the first time in a long time, I'm looking forward to what the future brings.

CHAPTER SEVEN

Tucker

FRIDAY NIGHT in Laurel Springs can sometimes get a little crazy, but nothing can remove the smile from my face. I looked at the letter from Karsyn before I left the house, and it's put a spring in my step.

"Tucker, come in."

The blaring sound of the radio indicates dispatch wants to speak to me. Hitting the button on my shoulder, I speak quietly, hoping she can take context clues. Sabrina is new, just hired in the last few months, but damn someone needs to give her a heads up she doesn't have to scream every time she talks to us.

"10-4, what do you need?"

It screeches again as she all but screams over the line.

"Cruise is requesting a dog to sniff his traffic stop. Can you respond? Ransom and Rambo are on lunch."

She still hasn't learned the ten codes either, but we

needed help and she was an applicant, so we'll take what we can get at this point.

"Show me as responding. I'll be there ASAP once you send the address over."

"Sorry." This time her voice is a little quieter. "I forgot that part."

"No biggie."

When I get the address, I turn my lights on, making Major bark in the back. He knows when lights flash and he can hear the sirens he's about to go do work. "You ready?" I look at him in the rearview.

If he could answer, I know he'd say yes. I've never had an animal be as in tune with my feelings as he is. Sometimes it's slightly disconcerting, but I know he'll have my back in any situation.

Once we get there, I groan inwardly. A car we've sniffed more than once is there. Not only that, but the guy sitting out next to it has run as well.

"What's going on?" I ask Cruise as I get Major out of the back.

The guy to the side yells. "This is profiling!"

Cruise ignores him. "There's an odor, and he refuses to admit to anything. She was driving, he was in the passenger seat."

"He's liable to run." I shake my head.

"Which is exactly why he's sitting next to that fence with handcuffs on," he says loud enough for the guy to hear.

"What, do you not want to run today, officers?" he taunts.

I turn to him. "Major could catch you, no issue. Do you want to get bit by a dog today? Because you take off, he won't let you go. He'll catch you. I know that without a doubt because I trained him."

"Is that a threat?"

Ignoring him, I pick up Major's leash, clicking my tongue at him. The tension is thick, and I want him to be able to do his job. "Let's do work. Find dope," I tell him. I lead him around the car and he does exactly what he's trained to do. He makes an indication, so I open the car door for him, allowing him to get in and search around. He makes another indication.

"Looks like there's something in there," I tell Cruise. "Feel free to look around."

"Good boy," I praise Major, giving him head rubs and putting him back in his spot.

When I make sure he's got water, and he's good, I walk over to where the guy and girl are handcuffed against the fence.

"You guys are always picking on me," he complains.

"You've run from me, dude," I laugh. "I've stopped you at least five times. All for reasons easily explained. You're a persistent offender."

"Only because you're constantly stopping me. Laurel Springs has a problem with me." He makes a noise in his throat.

"Laurel Springs wants you off their streets," I argue. "You're putting this shit out into the community. If you don't watch it, you'll be past rehabilitation, and then what the fuck are you going to do? Die in a drug house? That's where you're headed."

He grumbles again, Cruise calls me over. "Found heroin under her seat and crack in the passenger door."

Walking back over, I give the news to the two of them.

"Fuck that," the guy says. "It's all mine." He rolls his eyes.

"You're gonna take the fall for all of it?" I ask. "I mean

that's the manly thing to do, but then she's not gonna learn a lesson. The two of you are a huge problem for this area, and you both need help."

"Fuck it." He shifts on the ground. "I'll take it all. Come bail me out?" He looks at the girl beside him.

"You know I don't have any money," she whispers.

This is an argument the two of them will have to figure out. I'll never understand how these relationships make it work when there are drugs involved.

"You got this?" I question Caleb.

"Yup, thanks for your help."

I give him a wave before I get into my SUV and start making my rounds again.

Karsyn

"Mom, are you home?" I knock on the door, before pushing it in.

It's a bad habit she has, being at home with the door unlocked. I do the same with my car, but I never leave the door to my home unlocked. Too many things can happen if someone can get into your home.

"Hey, I'm out back," she yells.

Carefully I walk through the living room, not wanting to wake my dad up. He could sleep through an apocalypse, but I hate to ruin his slumber. He's a lineman for the local electric company, and I heard he was called out last night. If anyone deserves a little extra shuteye it's him.

When I get to the porch, I'm greeted by my mom's cat, who rubs against my legs. "Hey, Shadow." I bend down to give him a scratch on the head.

"What do I owe the pleasure?" she asks as she has a seat.

By the looks of things she's been planting flowers, which is her favorite thing to do. She weeds, replants, and comes up with new arrangements every freaking year. I think it's where I get my planner creativity from.

"Can't I just come visit you?" I have a seat next to her.

"You can, but that's not your normal way of doing things," she calls me on my shit.

I sigh, wondering how to start this, how in the world I can get through what I have to talk to her about.

"I met this guy," I start, running my fingers through my hair.

"This is good news, right?" She interrupts me.

"It is, but it's complicated."

"It always is, Karsyn. Spit it out."

The thing about my mom is she's never let me feel sorry for myself, even when it might be easier. Sometimes I love that about her, other times it gets on my damn nerves. Today, I'm not sure which.

"It's the same guy from before. The one who broke my heart. I know I told you I'd had my heart broken, but I didn't tell you about it. I wasn't ready. You and Dad were amazing back then, supporting me without even knowing what was going on. But Tucker was special. We spent months together, mostly just hanging out with one another. I fell in love." I shrug, pushing my hair behind my ear. "I told him, he left."

"Oh Kar." She reaches out, grabbing hold of my hand.

"I went into it with my eyes wide open, he told me what he wanted, and I just..." I'm at a loss for words.

"We can't help how we feel, Kar, sometimes things happen beyond our control."

A sigh works its way out of my throat. "So he's asked for another shot, and he's promised to be honest with me. The thing is, I need to be honest with him too." I look her deep in the eyes.

"Oh shit, you didn't tell him? You know you have to be honest with the people in your life."

"It's not just him." I reach out, taking a drink of her iced tea. "I haven't told anybody."

She gives me a disapproving stare. "Karsyn, you can't run from your past. It's made you who you are. How did you think you were going to explain it?"

"My past isn't easy to deal with," I protest. When people find out, they start looking at me differently, and that's when all my relationships go south, including friendships. They start treating me like I'm damaged goods, and I can't take it. It's why we moved here. For a new start, all the way around.

"For you." Her voice gentles. "It's not easy to deal with for you. You're not ever going to be the girl who had a normal childhood, as much as we tried to make it normal for you after it happened. It's just not in the cards for you. You've grown into an amazing woman. That's all a part of who you are."

"Mom, for once I don't want to be known as the little girl who was the focus of a manhunt across the state of Tennessee. He's a cop," I choke the words out.

She sighs. "*You* weren't the focus of the manhunt. The man who took you was. You have nothing to be ashamed of, and I'm sure as a man of the law, he knows that. If anyone can protect you from the dreams you have at night, it's him."

I know all of this, but I also know those forty-eight hours I was a kidnapped child have defined my whole life up until this point. I'm finally ready for something else to define me.

Tucker loving me fits that bill, but how will he feel to know I've kept this from him?

CHAPTER EIGHT

Karsyn

WHEN I GET to my apartment later that night, I'm a little uneasy. Maybe it's because Mom and I went into some things I haven't allowed to come to the surface in a long time, or maybe it's because talking about the incident always brings it back. Either way, I do a ritual I haven't done in years.

One of the things I insisted on when I moved here was that my apartment have a security system, and now I'm glad for it. Quickly I turn it off, thankful it was still set, but it doesn't give me the full feeling of safety I need tonight.

As I go through, I turn on every light, look in every hiding place, and force myself to open each closet door in turn. My hands shake as I get to the one in my room. My bottom lip trembles and I almost can't turn the knob, but I do.

Seeing it's empty is enough to make tears stream down my face.

"Karsyn." I bite my lip as I talk to myself. "You got over this a long time ago."

But did I really? It's never easy to get over traumatic events in your life, and mine was off the fucking scale. I stopped going to counseling years ago, and now I'm wondering if maybe I should give it a shot again.

Sighing, I go about my nighttime routine, even making myself take a shower, with the curtain half-way open.

"Stop being such a baby," I whisper, as I put my robe on, and then start to brush out my hair.

In my haste of wanting to get the shower over with, I didn't condition it, and it's going to be hell in the morning if I don't work it through tonight.

That's when I hear it.

A noise I'm not used to hearing.

My mind is going to every single thing this could be. It sounds like something is scraping against the window in my bedroom, and chances are it's a tree limb. Storms were expected to roll through Laurel Springs overnight. But I can't make myself believe that's all it is. I go everywhere, expecting the absolute worse.

When the noise is louder, I pull out my phone, making a call I haven't made in a long time. His deep voice is almost enough to calm me down itself.

"Tucker, I need you to come over. I'm scared."

"Are you okay?" He sounds panicked and I realize when he gets here he's going to think I'm an idiot, but I can't help the way I feel.

"I think so, but I can't be alone right now."

Those words are the most vulnerable I've ever spoken.

"Be right there."

He hangs up, and so do I. Waiting for him to get across

town to my apartment feels like the longest ten minutes of my life.

THE KNOCK on the door scares me, even though it shouldn't. I invited him over, and there's no reason to believe that the person knocking isn't Tucker.

"Who is it?" I ask as I pull my Ring doorbell app up on my phone.

"It's Tucker and Major."

There's a bark when he hears his name that makes me smile. I still wait to verify what he's said through the app on my phone, and I still open the door slowly after I see them on my phone.

"Are you okay?"

He doesn't barge his way in like I expected him to. He stands outside, hand on Major as he waits for my answer. It's a long couple of minutes while I try to figure out what to say, eventually I push some words from the dryness of my throat. "I got scared."

"I figured." He grins. "Now tell me what you got scared of, because I don't think I ever remember you being scared of anything."

Little does he know I'm scared of everything. "C'mon in."

They get inside, Major goes right to the place he used to sleep when he'd spend the night here before. Tucker? He stands in the middle of the room, commanding it like he does everything. He doesn't say anything and neither do I, but it's like he sees the look on my face. He holds his arms open and I run, throwing mine around him when he catches me.

"You're scaring me, Karsyn, tell me what's going on."

I can't, not yet, I just don't feel strong enough to. Instead, I work my hands around, up and under his t-shirt.

"Syn, come on."

"Just this once," I whisper, standing on tiptoe, brushing my lips across his jawline.

His body stands tightly still, trying to ignore my advances, but I know him and what makes him tick.

My fingers walk up his body to circle around his neck.

"What's going on here?" he whispers.

"I promise," I whisper back. "I'll tell you, but can you just make me feel good? For a little while?" Tears prick behind my eyes. "I miss you."

He misses me too, I know he does. That thought is confirmed when his hands slide down my body, cup my ass in his palms, and he walks me to my bedroom. He kicks the door shut, and turns, backing me up against it.

"I don't know what you're hiding from me," he mumbles as his mouth goes to work on my neck. "But after I get mine and you get yours, you're going to tell me. I've been patient, and I'll continue to be patient, Kar, but I need to know what I'm up against, what enemy I'm fighting."

"I'll tell you." I tilt my head back, giving him free reign of my neck.

With us it's always been like some porno, I know that's cliché, but it has been. Maybe that's what drew me to him; he's always known what he wants. Not that he used me, but he told me what he likes in the way he moans, grunts, and moves faster against my body. I've never had to wonder what makes him tick, because even though he's closed off on so many other things, he's an open book when it comes to the way he enjoys sex.

Out of nowhere our lips meet, and it's like an explosion of lust between the two of us. Our tongues tangle in an age-old dance, his cock presses deeply against my core as he pushes me harder against the wall. This is how I like *my Tucker*, hungry and ready for me.

My fingers and his fight over which ones will take off his shirt, and eventually he reaches behind him, pulling it up and over, before throwing it over to the side. He's gotten hotter since the last time we were together, looks like he's worked out some more. Muscles on his abs that had been there before are still there, but more surround them. I make a sound in my throat, running my fingers up and down his flesh.

"Had to do something," his deep voice speaks to me in the semi-darkness of the room. "Jerking it only sated my hunger for a while."

A blush works high onto my cheeks. This was something I'd almost forgotten about him, the way he loves to talk. If anyone could make a woman come just by uttering a few words, it's Tucker.

"I need you," I moan, pushing against him, hoping he drags me to the bed.

When he does, I almost trip over my feet in my eagerness to be with him. He sits me down on the bed in front of him, spreading my legs so he can stand between them. My bed is high off the ground, because I always want to see if someone is hiding under it. That's my own secret.

Because of the height, it puts us almost even with one another, when I'm sitting. He doesn't have to bend, I don't have to reach up, he can kiss me with this crazy pace that's both fast and slow. It's enough to drive me insane.

"Why?" I stick my fingers in the waistband of his jeans.

"Why are you making me wait?"

"Because I've wanted it so bad." He grins before leaning forward, grabbing hold of my shirt.

Getting that over my head, he presses me back against the blanket. I wait for precious seconds with my eyes closed, hoping he'll continue, but he doesn't. When I open my eyes, he's looking at me, almost like he can't believe I'm here with him.

"What?"

He rubs a hand over his mouth. "Just takin' this all in. I never thought I'd have you spread out like a goddamn buffet ever again."

I giggle slightly, but then his fingers touch my skin with the slightest brush. It's enough to bring ridges of gooseflesh across every inch he brushes.

"You like that?"

His dark eyes meet mine as his fingers head northward, to where my nipples are straining against the cups of my bra. Working where I do, I have to have the padded ones because we tend to keep it cold in the office. I nod, closing my eyes as his touch gets to the top of the lace edging.

"Let's see how much. I always hated you had to hide these tits while you worked."

He pulls the lace down, making a noise in his throat as he catches sight of my hardened nipples.

"Oh yeah." He leans forward at the waist, slightly blowing.

"Fuck," I groan. "Don't."

"You love to be teased, Karsyn, don't think I forgot that."

Right now I'm wishing he had, the only thing I want between my lets is him naked, and by the looks of things, I'll be waiting a long time for that tonight.

CHAPTER NINE

Tucker

IF THIS IS A DREAM, I one hundred percent don't want to wake up. I never gave up hoping I'd be right here between her legs again, but I didn't think it would be now. Because her bed is so high, I'm able to bend at the waist and situate my shoulders comfortably, grabbing her thighs, putting them over my shoulders.

She gasps. "Tucker."

"I'm gonna give you everything you deserve," I promise, burying my head in paradise. I don't ease in, like I know she assumes I will, because that's the way I've always been with her before. It's all been me easing her into who I am. Something clicked with me on the way over here. Maybe she didn't need me to be easy with her, maybe she wants me to be who I am.

So this is how I'm trying it this time. Hoping we're on the same page, and praying that she accepts the real Tucker. My tongue flicks at her clit, causing her to tighten her thighs around my head. Her hands move down her body, tangling in my hair, holding me tighter to her.

"Oh my God," she moans. Her body is strung tight, like she's trying to keep herself from reacting to what I'm doing.

I pull my mouth back from her. "Don't hold back, Karsyn. Give it all to me."

She opens her eyes, looking down her body at me. This is one of the sexiest things she could have ever done. It gives me a look at her vulnerability, the way her eyes turn dark with her arousal. Normally so light, they look like she's been overtaken with the Devil himself. A switch flips in her when I give her permission to be the woman she is. Her fingers dig deeper into my hair, as short as it is, she's managing to tug on it.

"Do it again." She opens her thighs wider.

Smirking, I bury my head deeper, growling when she starts thrusting against my face, riding the crest of my tongue and going after every bit of her pleasure. This shit is hot. This woman in my arms the sexiest I've ever had. Releasing the flesh of her leg, I get my fingers involved, thrusting them along with my tongue. Helping her ride the edge of passion.

"Don't stop," she begs. "Please don't stop."

I don't even let go of her clit to tell her I'm not going to. I just keep working her harder and harder. Wanting her to get hers first.

"Fuck, Tucker". She presses harder against me, clasps her thighs tighter around me, and that's when I feel her let go. She's moaning and making these noises that go straight to my cock.

I don't even remember getting out of my jeans and boxer briefs, but the next thing I know, I'm covering her body with mine, tonguing her nipples as she shakes. "You still on birth control?" I question before twirling my tongue around her flesh.

"Yes," she answers on a sigh.

"Nobody else since you." I push myself up on my arms, pulling my knees under me.

Her eyes meet mine, and her arms go up over her head to grip the edge of the bed. Lining my cock up with her, I tease her slightly, wetting the tip with her juices before I slowly slide in. "Ohhhh," she moans.

"God." I let the oath slip out as I sink myself balls deep inside her.

We both still for a moment, allowing ourselves to get reacquainted with one another. I feel the resistance in her pussy let go, and then I start my rhythm. The two of us, we know each other well. I press my thumb to her clit as I work in and out of her body, she runs a hand up and down my lower abdomen. The bed squeaks as I push in, pull out.

"Still didn't get this thing fixed?" I grin down at her.

"No reason to." She grins back.

That answer makes my heart lift. Maybe I didn't fuck things up as badly as I thought. Lowering my body down over hers, I wrap my arms around her back, rolling over so that she's on top.

Her long hair flows down her body, covering those tits of hers. "Ride me." I grab hold of her hips, helping her find her rhythm. This is something she wasn't always comfortable doing. She didn't always like showing this vulnerable side of herself, but as we got to know one another and as we got more comfortable, we started to do things with one another we'd never done with anyone else.

She cants her hips against mine, moving up and down, her stomach tightens and loosens, tightens and loosens, as she goes for hers. When I steady her with my strong grip, her hands go up into her hair, holding it above her head. The motion lifts her tits so they set high and proud against her chest. I push her hips down onto my length, hold her there, and press up, hammering into her. The movement makes her gasp, falling on top of me. I grip her around the waist, turning her over again so that I'm on top again.

She grins up at me, her eyes glazed with passion. She's smiling so sweetly, and I can see it in her eyes. The love she's always had for me. I halt my thrusting, looking down at her. "I love you," I mouth, because I can't give voice to the words yet.

She nods, wrapping me up in her arms. My weight on my forearms, I wrap them around the top of her head and thrust again, setting the rhythm that will finally get me off. My fingers tug on the root of her hair, knowing she likes a little hair pulling.

Her hand sneaks between us, rubbing against her clit. "I'm gonna come, Tucker, gonna come."

"Come on," I encourage her. "One more time."

"Oh, oh, oh," she moans before she thrusts up into me, throwing her head back against the bed. I bury mine in her neck, trying to keep my shit together.

With superhuman strength I stop, letting her ride out what will probably be her final orgasm. Sweat covers both our bodies, and her chest is heaving against mine. I struggle to sit on my knees, but somehow I manage it, pressing her thighs farther apart, gritting my teeth as I pound home. My cock hardens even further, lengthening as it searches for its release.

Every muscle in my body is pulled tight as I ride her. "Oh my God." I close my eyes as I thrust into her, pressing down on her thighs, wanting nothing more than to finally come. But I'm not there yet. Right on the edge, not yet pushed over, it's a hell of a place to be. Each part of me is ready for it, wants it more than anything. Chasing it, I pull out, push in, grasp the flesh of her thighs in my fingers, and use it to fuck her. Opening my eyes, I take one last look of her before I close them again, throw my head back and don't stop thrusting until I come.

"Oh my God." My breath is stuttered as I get closer. "Yes, yes, yes," I chant, knowing this will be the culmination of so much wanting, wishing, praying that life was different.

Bottoming out, I finally come, holding her thighs tightly down on me as I empty inside her. It's a relief I've never felt before, a lifting of not only my balls, but my spirit. Almost as if all the bad shit I've been dealing with pours out of my body, cleansing me, cleansing us, letting us move forward without all this shit in between us. I collapse on top of her, breathing heavily. She runs her hands up and down my body, cradling me in the comfort of her arms.

"I missed this," I whisper as I try to regulate my heart rate. "I missed you holding me after this."

She laughs. "I always thought you hated it because you couldn't seem to get out of my arms fast enough."

"It makes me vulnerable," I admit. "I've never been vulnerable for anyone except for you."

Her lips land on my forehead, kissing me softly. As her fingers make circles on my flesh, I can't tell she's thinking. Maybe it's about what she wanted to tell me, maybe it isn't. I hope sooner rather than later she tells me what I'm fighting, but I also know from my experience as a law enforcement officer, you can't rush these things.

It could be fifteen minutes or maybe an hour later when

she readjusts herself underneath me, and takes a deep breath. "I always wondered what we would be doing when I finally told you," she starts.

I hold still because I don't want her to stop. In my experience, you can easily spook someone and they'll just stop talking. I want her to talk to me, I want to know all her secrets and fears.

"Never thought it would be like this." She digs her nails into my skin slightly. "I tried to convince myself it didn't matter that I hadn't been completely honest with you, and then tonight happened. I now know I have to come clean. When I was thirteen I was kidnapped," she whispers. "For two days there was a manhunt in Tennessee for me and the man who took me."

As the realization of what she's said washes over me, I have no words.

CHAPTER TEN

Karsyn

HE ISN'T SAYING anything and that's maybe the scariest thing about this situation. I've never known Tucker to be a man of no words. Few words? Yes. More often than not, but speechless? Never. The longer he stays quiet, the more disconcerting it is.

"You're gonna have to explain this to me babe, what the fuck happened?" He pulls away from me, pushing himself up into a sitting position.

I sit up too, grabbing the sheet up to shield my nakedness from him. I'm about to lay myself vulnerable and the comfort is needed. The breath I take isn't nearly deep enough, but it will have to do. "We lived in Tennessee," I start. "Jackson, and my dad was working for an aluminum plant. Mom was staying at home back then, but that day she had a doctor's appointment. Thirteen was old enough for me to stay by myself, obviously." I grin.

He smirks. "I think I was staying by myself at six."

"You've always been an overachiever."

We're quiet for a few minutes as I think about how I want to continue. So many things that day could have gone differently, and for a long time I thought about my part in what happened. I took more of the blame than my parents did, and for years I struggled under the burden of inadvertently causing this to myself.

"It was okay for me to go to my best friend's house two streets over," I start again. "I had to call my dad at work and let him know if I couldn't get in touch with my Mom. Since she was at the doctor's office, she wasn't answering her cell phone. Dad worked in the offices at the aluminum plant, and I guess that day he had meetings, because he didn't answer either." Tucker starts rubbing my hand as I play with a string on my comforter. "I got impatient. I'd called five times and left five messages, I'd called my mom three times and left three messages. My best friend had a new puppy and I badly wanted to see it."

"Any kid would have wanted to see it." Tucker gives me the support I didn't even know I needed.

"I loved puppies, still do, but back then, Mom and Dad wouldn't let me have a pet. Which meant everyone else's I adopted as my own too. Neither one of them had answered and I was done waiting."

"So what did you do?"

That day is both clear and hazy in my mind. There are some parts I can remember like they were yesterday, other parts, I must have blocked from my memory.

"Grabbed my backpack, locked the house up, and took off for my friend's. I wasn't going to be denied any longer."

"You're still the same today, ya know?" He moves his hand up to my jawline, cupping it and pushing his fingers back into my hair. "You go after what you want, and hardly ever let anyone stand in your way. You're a strong force of nature, Karsyn."

"For a long time after this, I wasn't." I shake my head. "I just couldn't seem to figure out who I was. But I'm getting ahead of myself."

"I'm ready for the rest if you wanna give it to me."

"Normally I would have taken a shortcut through the back of our yards, but one of our neighbors was doing construction on their back deck, and it messed up my normal path. This day I took the main road. I didn't like the main road because people drove like idiots, and I was always scared I'd be hit."

In my mind, I go back to that day. It's weird the things that stand out. The heat of the sun, the smell of the grass, the chirping of the birds. It was a perfect day, nothing warned me it would turn into what it did.

"I was about four houses away from mine when I noticed the truck behind me." Goosebumps raise on my flesh, and a dark foreboding overtakes me the way it always does. "I have no idea how long it'd been following me. I wasn't the type of girl to take in my surroundings. My parents hadn't taught me to be watchful, they didn't teach me to be respectfully scared of people. I mean we lived in a nice neighborhood, and back then maybe we thought we were safer? I don't know. But I noticed him. I walked faster, and he sped up. I walked slower, and he slowed down. He didn't ever get completely even with me. He stayed either slightly behind or slightly in front of me. I was getting nervous. My heart was pounding and I was scared. I hoped there was a neighbor outside, but this was summer and everybody was either at work or on vacation. I thought about leaving the main road and going back through the yards, but I didn't know if I had gotten to the house with the construction yet." Tears start streaming down my face. "In my panic, I couldn't remember whose house it was. Isn't that stupid? I'd lived there my whole life, had walked through those yards for years, and in that moment I couldn't remember."

"It's normal." Tucker wipes at the moisture. "It's perfectly normal. Happens to everybody."

"As I turned onto the road my friend lived on, I had to stop, a car was turning too sharply and I stopped to avoid them. Some teenager who didn't know how to drive yet, and didn't realize what was going on. I remember thinking, can't he see I'm scared? Couldn't he have just stopped? Me stopping gave the guy all the time it took. He stopped the truck, reached out, and grabbed me. I screamed, threw my backpack at him, and ran. He was taller and the backpack was no match for him. Within steps he had me, his hand over my mouth and I was in his truck with him."

"Don't scream again." He flashed a knife at me. "I'll show you how easy it is to carve up flesh."

"That scared me enough that I didn't say a peep, not when my best friend stood outside her house, watching as we drove away. I waved at her, hoping she would see what was happening, and praying someone would help."

"What did he do?" Tucker's jaw is tight and I know it's not because he's mad at me, he's furious at the situation. I was too.

This is the hardest part to talk about.

"He took me to a nearby motel and made me change clothes." I close my eyes as I remember the embarrassment I felt.

"Smart, he didn't want people looking for you in the

clothes you were wearing. Which means he probably had a history."

I nod; he did have a history, and we would find out this wasn't the first time he'd taken a girl.

"He touched me when I changed," I whisper. "I was an early bloomer and was wearing a training bra at eleven."

"Did he do anything else?" he asks just as softly. "Besides touching you?"

"No." I shake my head. "I think he would have, but he dyed my hair and while we were waiting on it to be done, he turned on the TV. There was already an Amber Alert out for me," I sob slightly. "My friend had seen what happened and told her mom. They even had the license plate number."

"Good friend."

"Yeah, she was the best."

How do I tell him the kidnapping ruined more than one life? That's neither here nor there right now, and I don't have to get into everything tonight, I remind myself.

"What did he do?"

"Freaked out. I think he had been planning to hole up in the hotel, but now that the cops had his license plate number and the make of the truck, he was fucked. He washed the dye out of my hair so fast that it didn't even take, it just gave me streaks," I run my fingers through my hair. "It's why I don't get highlights to this day. He packed us up quick, and then we snuck down to the parking lot. He stole an SUV. And then he was hiding me in the back while we hit the highway."

"Damn, Karsyn. Out of everything you could have told me, this wasn't even on my radar."

"I know." I nod. "But I can't ask you to be honest with me about stuff and then not tell you about this experience that completely changed my life. For two straight days we were on the run. He touched me again a few times, and threatened to kill me more than once. As we hit Knoxville, the Tennessee Highway Patrol was onto us. We ended up getting into a wreck."

Which is a fucking understatement. We were lucky we weren't killed.

"He's been in prison since then, and every time he's up for parole, I go tell my story."

"You're strong." He leans in, kissing me softly. "And I don't deserve you. Not after the shit you've been through and the shit I've put you through."

CHAPTER ELEVEN

Tucker

I HAVEN'T SLEPT since Karsyn told me her story. She's sleeping soundly wrapped in my arms. There's no way I'm going to let go today. Never mind the fact I have to be on-shift in about three hours. Without disturbing her, I reach over, grabbing my phone. Ransom owes me a favor.

T: I'm calling in that favor where I worked twenty-four hours so you could go home and fuck your wife on your anniversary.

R: Screw you, we make love.

I knew that would get him all fired up.

T: Fine, I worked twenty-four hours so you could go home and make love to your wife. Either way, I'm calling in the favor.

R: Is everything okay?

Ransom knows me, and he knows I honestly never call in

favors, it's just not the type of guy I am. If I'm actually calling in on a favor, something serious has happened.

T: I'm with Karsyn. Some things have gone down and I need to stay with her. I really appreciate this.

R: Hopefully good things, I know you miss her. No problem, you always work with me, I'm happy to work with you. Believe it or not, I'm psyched you're spending time with her.

This isn't Ransom and my normal conversation, but I appreciate the fact he truly knows the type of man I am.

T: I have. Thanks for this.

R: Name your first kid Ransom and we're even.

A chuckle escapes my lips before I throw my cell phone over to the bedside table again. Knowing I have nowhere to be, I wrap my arms tighter around Karsyn, and finally fall to sleep.

"TUCKER." I hear the soft whisper, feel the tips of her fingers on my face. "Tucker."

I would know that voice anywhere. I clear my throat as I bury my face in hers. "Do I have to get up?" I stretch against her.

She giggles as my breath hits her skin. It's one of her most ticklish spots and I've used it to my advantage more than once.

"Yes, Major is starving. I know you probably have some

food in your truck, but I didn't want to go through your stuff to find your keys."

At the sound of his name, Major hops on the bed, whining softly. I reach down with my hand, gently rubbing his nose. "Sorry, bud, I didn't mean for that to happen. I bet you need to go out too."

"I tried to get him to go for me, but he wouldn't." Karsyn scoots closer to me.

"Sometimes he's picky."

"I seem to remember that about both of you." She trails her fingernail along my chest.

Finally opening my eyes, I reach out, grabbing her finger. "It's a personality quirk." I kiss her jawline.

"Is that what we're calling it now?"

Sitting up, I rub my eyes with the heels of my hands. "That's what it is, babe. That's all it is."

"Mmm hmmm." She purses her lips.

It's then that I realize she's put clothes on. "When did we decide to get dressed?"

She looks up at me, her hazel eyes dancing. "When I decided to try and get your dog to go out for me. Didn't think it was appropriate to go out there naked.

I agree, I don't necessarily want a ton of people to see her the way I do. This right here, is mine. "Good call. Are you hungry?"

"Starving." She rubs her stomach.

"Let's go grab some food." Picking up my cell phone, I whistle at how late it is. I'm usually an early riser. "Looks like we'll have to make that lunch."

Karsyn gives me a look, and I'm not sure what to make of it. It's one-part disbelief and another part shock. "Are you okay?"

She sighs, sitting up in the bed, holding Major's head in her lap. "Is this because of what I told you last night? You're one of those protectors." She grins. "You always want people to be safe, and you'll go out of your way to do that."

"You're asking if all I'm doing is protecting you? Like that's the reason why I'm in bed with your right now?" This is irritating, but I have to remember where we came from. Our relationship before was almost purely physical. We didn't share feelings, until she blurted hers out one night and maybe that was where we went wrong. Maybe we need to share how we feel.

"I can't get my heart broken this time," she twirls her hair and says softly. "I want to go into this with my eyes wide open, Tuck. You can't blame me for it. You wrecked me when you left before."

I know I did. I not only wrecked her, but I wrecked myself. The department therapist would call me on all of my shit and tell me I'm really good at self-sabotage, but I refuse to be this time. "I'm all in if you are."

"As simple as that?"

"As simple as that." I reach over, grabbing her hand. "I get it, you don't believe me, and I understand why. I've grown up, matured, and realized what it means to be a person capable of love since we were last together."

"You broke me." She stops twirling her hair, standing up straighter. It's almost like she transforms in front of my eyes. She doesn't mince words.

"I broke myself," I assure her. "There were days when I didn't want to get out of bed because of what I did, Karsyn. I knew within days I had fucked it up."

"Which is why you started following me?" She laughs.

"No, I had to work on myself first. There were things I

had to deal with, figuring out why I felt unworthy of your love, why it's so hard for me to say the words. I'm still working on it, but I'm sick of not having you in my life. I'd much rather struggle with you, than without you."

"I'll be patient," she promises. "I know I wasn't before, I wanted everything all at once. I didn't allow you to ease in, because I didn't know how you were feeling, but we can change that. As long as you're open with me, we can make this work."

"Can we?" I know most of that is up to her. I'm the one who gave up before, so I need her to be willing to give me that chance.

"We can, we'll be adults about this, and not run before we walk. We'll communicate and not assume."

"We're the worst at that," I remind her. It's what fucked us up the first time.

"Then that's where we'll spend most of our time. Figuring out our languages of love."

We laugh as we look at one another. Slowly I get serious, letting the smile fall off of my face. Leaning over I cup her cheek in my palm. "I can't lose you again, Syn. My life had no color, my soul had no purpose, and fuck it was lonely."

"I don't wanna lose you again either. We can do this, Tucker."

"But first, lunch?"

She laughs. "But first lunch!"

Major barks his approval and reluctantly I let her out of my arms so that we can get dressed to start our day. I've not been around a woman getting ready for her day since the two of us were together, and I have to admit this is something I missed more than I thought I would.

There's something about standing with her at the dual

sinks in her apartment. Me brushing my teeth while she brushes hers. I sneak glances at her out of the corner of eye. Watch as she puts lotion on her hands, something on her face, and sighs when she looks at her hair.

"I'm thinking of getting it cut." She looks over at me. "It gets in the way, and I always do like one or two things with it. But I also like having it long. It was a process to grow out. I'm kind of undecided. What do you think?"

The image of her straddling me, holding her hair up in her hands as her stomach rocks against mine flashes through my memories just like a movie. Without the hair piled up on top of her head, it just wouldn't be the same.

"Don't. I love the way it tangles up when we're getting intimate, I like running my fingers through it when you've put your head on my chest, and I want to bury my face in it so I can smell the shampoo you use. The scent of your shampoo always reminds me of home."

Her eyes shine bright in the dim lighting. "Damn, Tuck. When you get serious, you get serious."

Nodding my head, I grab the end of one of the locks, holding it in between my fingers. "I do, and I've been serious about you for a long time. I just didn't want to admit it."

"You can be vulnerable with me, you know."

"I know, I just was. It took a lot for me to say those words."

She grins. "Then I'll hold them close to my heart and never let them go."

This girl, she kills me and challenges me. For the first time in years, Tucker Williams wants to be a good man. The best man.

All for Karsyn Fallaway.

"I think I'll keep it long," she whispers.

"I think I like that."

Another stolen glance at one another is made before we finish our morning routines. And just like that, I'm right where I wanna be.

CHAPTER TWELVE

Karsyn

"STOP!" I giggle, grinning widely as I slap my hand on top of Tucker's as it trails up my bare thigh. "I'm trying to get this done." I point to my laptop. "And you're not making it very easy."

"It's not my job to make it easy," his deep voice teases. "I'm supposed to distract you."

"Well it's working, but we have to get this message out so that we can get the ball rolling on the fundraisers," I remind him. "Not like you've thought anything about it."

He moves his hand farther down my thigh, an innocent expression covering his face. "Can't blame me. I mean you've been sitting here in just my t-shirt for hours. Sooner or later, I'm going to want to see what you have under it."

I try to bite back my smile because I don't want him to know how much this affects me. The truth is my heart is soaring, my stomach pitching with the thrill of excitement. It wasn't like this before. He wasn't completely open with his feelings; I felt his attraction, but I never felt his affection. "If you help me with this, maybe I'll show you myself."

His dark eyes go darker. "Is that a promise?"

"Maybe it is." I give him a smirk.

"What do we need to do?"

A full-body laugh escapes my chest. It takes so little for him now. "Can you ask Ransom if we can use him and Rambo?"

"On it." He's already got his phone out, texting.

I finish writing all my emails, sending them out to the proper people, and lean over, marking it off on my to-do list.

"Are we done?" he asks.

"We are."

"Where's Major?" He looks around for his dog.

"He's in the kitchen. He fell asleep on the air conditioner vent."

He snickers, shaking his head. "He does love to be chilly."

"A lot like you."

Tucker situates himself on the couch so that I'm below him, cradling his body in between my thighs. Unlike the feverish pace of last night, this is decidedly slow. His hands mold to my thighs, pushing up against my flesh, lifting the fabric of the shirt up at a snail's pace. His eyes are hooded as he leans into me, our lips meeting just as slow as his hands on my thighs. The kiss is relaxed, lazy. Gently coaxing my lips apart, the feeling of his tongue sliding in gives me goose bumps. His mouth on mine is a slow fuck making my nipples peak underneath the cotton material their straining against. My fingers grab for his shoulders, denting his skin as he smears his lips against my jawline and then down to my neck, licking, sucking, biting at the sensitive flesh.

"Tucker," I sigh, lifting my core against him.

The only thing preventing us from coming together are his boxer briefs and my panties, but those don't even feel like barriers. He's thrusting his cock toward me, simulating sex as his mouth moves down my body. Throwing my head back against the arm of the couch, I close my eyes and give myself over to him. I trust him to assuage the ache now taking over my entire body. A moan works its way out as I feel his tongue sweep against the cotton of this shirt, before biting it through the material. It's both muted and sharp at the same time. My fingernails bite into his flesh now, moving up to his neck, my hands cup his head, holding him firm to where I want him.

We're rocking against one another, still slow, as he lifts the shirt up to my rib cage, right under where my breasts sit. There's a huge part of me that doesn't want him to let go. There's another part that desperately wants him to.

"Open," he whispers.

My eyes are slits as I look down to my mouth. His thumb and forefinger are there. I do ask he asks, opening and taking those two fingers inside, licking them like I would his cock.

He growls, letting go of my nipple before pushing the shirt up and over my tits. Pulling his fingers from my mouth, he uses them to twist my left nipple as his mouth takes my right.

"Please," I beg, needing to feel him inside me. My hands go down his back to his waist, slipping my palms under the fabric of his boxer briefs, digging my nails into his ass.

Before I know what's happened, the shirt is off, the panel of my panties is pulled aside, and he's slipped his cock out of the top of his underwear. When he pushes home I sigh, because my God, I feel like I've waited forever.

Tucker lets out a guttural groan, his eyes meeting mine.

"God, I missed you," he whispers before he leans forward, taking my mouth with his.

We kiss, hungry and sloppy as he thrusts in and pulls out, pushing me closer to the pinnacle. When he stops, pulls out, and stands, I'm not sure what's happening, but I watch as he pushes his underwear down his body, and pulls mine off too. He stands behind me, snaking his arm around my chest. His hands palm my tits, his mouth goes to the back of my neck, and I groan, surrounded by him. "Fuck," I breathe, not sure how I'm supposed to handle this side of him. When he gets this way it's all encompassing and I love it.

He presses me down on the couch, making sure the pillow I have there isn't suffocating me. His hands tilt my hips up slightly, rubbing over the skin of my ass. A sharp slap makes me gasp, before he lowers himself down, slipping his cock in between my thighs and thrusts home.

"Tucker, oh my God," I moan as he puts his arms on either side of me, boxing me in with the weight and strength of himself.

His voice is deep, sexy, and everything I love about him as he mutters a *fuck*. Together we rock back and forth, straining against one another.

"You feel so good," he grunts as he pumps harder, faster inside of me.

"You do too," I answer his grunt with one of my own when he pushes a little rougher than I've grown accustomed to.

Looking to the side, I see his thumb, held up to help him keep his balance. My mouth salivates, I just want to touch him. Reaching forward with my head, I capture it in my mouth. Running my tongue up and down it, around the tip, just like I do to his cock, sucking gently.

"Shit," he breathes out, pushing himself up on his knees, using his other hand to smack my ass again. "Yes, suck it like you suck my dick," he encourages.

All I need to hear is that he's enjoying himself, that's all I've ever needed to hear. I feel like a fucking sex kitten when he's encouraging me. There's nothing that makes me feel better, makes me feel sexier. I always want to give everything to him, show him I can be the woman he needs.

As his palm connects with my ass again, I feel myself tumbling over the edge, letting go, and gripping him tightly.

"Son of a bitch," he moans. "That's it, Syn, come for me." He thrusts harder. "Come. For. Me."

Finally I have to let go of his thumb, and I scream loudly as he gives me the last three thrusts hard, just the way I like them. On the third one, I feel the heat inside my body, him coming hard.

"Oh fuck," he moans, pulling out as another pulse splatters against my back.

His body drops against mine, breathing heavily in my ear.

"You're gonna kill me," I sigh loudly.

"Negative, Fallaway, you're gonna kill me one day. I'm older."

I giggle. "But you're in much better shape."

"I don't know." He disentangles our bodies, rising on his arms. When he does, he scoots down, biting my ass cheek. "This looks pretty rock-solid to me."

"We have a mess." I look behind me, pointedly at him.

"Don't look at me, you started this, wearing my shirt and shit."

"Oh." I raise my eyebrows. "So that's all it takes."

"Yes." He levers himself up off the couch.

He walks toward the kitchen, and I allow myself to close my eyes, let my body rest for a moment. Truth is, I can hardly believe this is my life after the last year. How did this happen? Am I setting myself up to get hurt again?

I push those thoughts out of my head, reminding myself I can hurt him as much as he can hurt me. *We're both all in.* That will be my mantra.

"Here." He uses paper towels to wipe off my back. "After this, we'll go shower."

My legs protest as he helps me up from the couch. "No funny business in the shower, I don't think I can take it."

He pulls me close, his eyes dark again. This time though, not with passion, with a seriousness I haven't seen from him yet. "None of this is funny, Karsyn, I promise."

Lifting up on my toes, I kiss him, softly, slowly. "I know, if you notice, I'm not laughing. I feel it too."

"It's scary." He swallows roughly. "But if I'm going to be scared with anyone, it'll be with you."

Hand in hand we walk to my bathroom, and I know that in the future, I'll look back on this day as a turning point.

I just didn't realize how close that future was to us.

CHAPTER THIRTEEN

Tucker

"THANKS FOR TAKING my shift the other night." I clap Ransom on the back as we meet in the conference room. I'm coming on-shift and he's going off. It's customary for us to have a meeting at least once a week.

"No problem, I owed you." His eyes look me over. "Whatever happened, it looks good on you. I take it you and Karsyn are working things out?"

"Trying to." I nod. "You know as well as anyone else that it isn't always that easy.

"Nothing worth it ever is." He yawns. "Like parenthood."

"Up all night?"

"Not all night, but a few times. I took over so that Stella could sleep. Keegan's getting his nights and days mixed up, especially with the hours we're working. It's hard to keep him on a schedule." He runs a hand through his hair. "And this one," he looks down at Rambo, "gets all worried when Keegan's worried. So then I have to deal with him."

"They're only little for a while," I remind him.

"I know." He grins. "He's trying to walk, and I'm like dude, slow down."

"He can't even crawl yet," I laugh.

He gives me a look. "Like it would surprise you if my kid walks before he crawls?"

He's right, it really won't.

Menace stands in front of the group. "If we could get this meeting going? I got places to be."

We give him our attention, heading for our seats.

"HOW ARE you doing with the fundraiser?" Menace asks as we're leaving.

"Good, we've made contact with a few people who are willing to help. Karsyn's got a schedule of what we're doing, and she'll be sharing it at the next LSERT meeting. We're just waiting on a few more people. It's looking good though. I think we'll also have some donations from a few families, and that will help too."

"Have y'all approached Blaze? I'm sure her organization could throw in a little," he reminds me.

"Oh no, that's a good idea. I'll be sure and have Karsyn do that."

Menace smirks. "Having her do all the asking?"

"She's nicer than I am."

"Spending a lot of time together."

I roll my eyes. "Not you too."

"I'm a certified romantic. You've met my wife."

They are the couple everyone wants to be. "I have met your wife, and I have no doubt she doesn't allow you to be anything else other than romantic."

"So answer my question. Are you spending a lot of time together? Is it working out for you? Knowing that my men are happy is a big part of this job. If you're unhappy, that's when things can go sideways. It's in my best interesting to know how things are going."

Or you're just nosey, I want to add, but I get it. "We are spending time together," I admit. "We're trying to work things out, but I seriously fucked up."

"It won't be your last time," he laughs. "No seriously, I know this about every guy. We always fuck up some way or another. It's about trying to figure out how to make it work after we fuck up."

Rubbing the back of my neck, I grimace. "That's what I'm trying to do. Figure out how to get past the part where I fucked up. I mean she told me she loved me, Mason, and I left."

His eyes widen. "What?"

"Yeah, I mean I hurt her in ways I'm not even sure I comprehended before."

"That's tough."

"It is, but I'm doing my best. I'm trying to be the man she deserves."

He claps me on the shoulder. "Sometimes we just are the men our ladies deserve. We can try to be perfect and things don't work out. We can fuck up and think there's absolutely no repairing it, but in the end we're meant to be with them. That's what you have to believe."

I appreciate what he's saying, but I'm not sure I'm that person for her. She seems to think I am, so I'm willing to try.

I'm willing to do anything for Karsyn, but I can't hurt her again. Hurting her will kill me.

PULLING UP AT THE CAFÉ, I see Nick's cruiser. The two of us are meeting for a what amounts to a late-shift lunch. Parking next to him, I let Major out of the SUV, and grab his leash to walk into the restaurant. He waves me over to a booth in the back. It's one where we both sit facing the door.

"What's up?" I ask as I scoot in on the other side of the circular design.

"Coffee, lots of coffee. Ella decided it was time to play, all day today." He shakes two sugar packets before opening them and putting them into his coffee.

"You and Ransom both seem to be having the same issues."

"Yeah? I haven't talked to him in a few days. This is recent with Ella. Been happening since Spring Break, when Kels had the week off and D was off from school. We didn't keep the schedule. We all kinda stayed up at all hours, and now we're regretting it."

Our waitress comes over getting our orders. I get my shot of caffeine from a glass of Coke, and I order for Major too. We're sitting in silence. That's what I like most about Nick. He doesn't have to be talking all the damn time. He's okay sitting in silence, when most everyone else always has to be talking. I appreciate it more than he knows. Tonight though, the silence is giving me things to think about.

"How do you do it?"

"Do what?"

We normally don't get into each other's business and I feel slightly awkward with what I'm about to ask him, but it matters. So fucking much. "How do you make it work? Having a family, doing this job, making time for everything. How does it work?"

He tilts his head to the side, giving me a smile. "It's easy; I can't imagine not having my family in my life. I ran from it, for a long time."

"I remember you and Kels had a hard time getting together."

He shakes his head. "It wasn't that, it was me admitting how much I needed her in my life. Had I done that in the beginning, I would have saved us so much heartbreak. Why are you asking?"

Our food arrives and I busy myself fixing my burger the way I like it, ignoring his question for as long as I'm able. "What if I wanted a life with Karsyn?"

The look he gives me goes straight to my soul, almost like he can tell exactly what I'm feeling. "Do you? Want a life with Karsyn?"

It's time to be honest, to cut the bullshit and admit to someone what the fuck I'm feeling. If I can admit it to him, maybe then I can admit it to myself and then to her. "Yeah, I do. It took me by surprise," I sigh. "I never thought I was the type of guy who'd want a woman to be a part of my life, but here I am."

He takes a drink of his coffee, sitting it down with a grimace. "I hate that shit, but it's the only thing that gets me through. Do you know my reason for getting through? My wife and kids. I was a lot like you, Tucker. A lot like you. I didn't think what I have now was for me. I fought it every step of the way, and then I got what I didn't even know I wanted. It's hard, everything but the loving them part. They're easy to love, I just had to open myself up to it."

"That's the easy part?" Surely he doesn't understand the kind of anxiety I'm having over that statement.

"It is," he assures me. "She loves you, love her back. That's all she's asking."

"Be vulnerable like that? I've never allowed myself to be."

"Welcome to your new life, Tucker. You give her what she needs, she'll give you the entire world. Let yourself love her. Have you told her?"

It's embarrassing to admit this. "I mouthed it to her while we were having sex."

"Jesus man," he laughs. "You're a mess."

"I am, I don't know if I'm actually the right person for her, but she says I am."

"Do you love her?" he asks, and I stare at him dumbfounded.

"If someone held a gun to her head, what goes through your mind?" he presses.

"My life - both with and without her."

"Without her, how does that life feel?"

I don't even have to think. "Empty, lonely. Exactly what I've been living this last year."

"Do you want that for the rest of your life?"

God no, that's my worst nightmare. Knowing I won't have her to wake up with, to talk to before I go to sleep. This past year I've been walking around like a shell of my former self, trying to figure out how to get that Tucker back. The time I spent with her the last few days? I felt like that old Tucker, the one who knew what life was like. The one who wasn't afraid of being lonely.

"No, I want the rest of my life to be filled with her and whatever type of family we make. I want a Christmas Tree with her and Major in front of it."

"Then go for it, Tuck. You make it work. You want it bad enough? You just make it work."

The answer seems so simple - but I would learn it was anything but.

Nick's phone vibrates on the table. He smirks, before he picks it up presumably answering the person on the other end. "I need to make a pit stop."

"Oh yeah?"

"Yeah, my girl needs me."

"Which one?" I joke.

"The older one is afraid the little one won't eat when it comes time. She's been fussy all the way around. We don't have shit going on, so I'm going to make a pit stop." He picks up his cup, draining it. "If you wanna see your girl, you should come with me. She's at my house."

"Yeah?" This is good news for me, considering my shift is over in about thirty minutes.

"Yep. You should just follow me on over."

"I could do that."

He laughs. "Your welcome. Ya know for all. The advice and making sure you get booty calls and such."

I flip him off. "I'll say thank you when you actually do something I can thank you for."

CHAPTER FOURTEEN

Karsyn

"AND I WAS THINKING," Darren says as he shows me some of the designs he's made. "That if we could get a paw print of both Rambo and Major, we could burn it into these plaques."

"Burn it?" I ask. This kid isn't even old enough to drive yet, and he's lost me already.

"Yeah, we can get one print from each of them, cast it, and then make a transferrable copy that I can burn into the wood."

I'm still lost, I look to Kelsea for help.

"You know, those tables you like at the flea market? They're made that way," she says as she struggles with Ella. "C'mon, El, eat. We messed up our sleep schedule and it's been hell," she sighs.

"She wants Dad." Darren rolls his eyes good-naturedly. "She hates the rest of us right now."

"She doesn't hate us," Kelsea argues. "I'm her mom."

I snort loudly. "She'll eventually hate you for one thing or another."

"What do you think?" Darren asks, looking at me for approval. "Should I make them?"

The one I'm holding in my hand looks damn good. "Yeah." I nod, decision made. "Make fifty, we'll sell them at the Meet and Greet we're planning."

"How many people have said yes to the Meet and Greet?" Kelsea asks, as she tries again to get Ella to eat.

"Everyone we've asked so far, it's definitely a go. We just have to verify with the LSPD what date is good for them."

That's when Ella screams bloody murder. She's had enough of whatever Kelsea's doing to her. In the middle of the excitement, the front door opens and in comes Nick, with Tucker on his heels.

"What's with all the screaming?" Nick grins, going directly for his daughter. "Why's such a pretty girl making so much noise?"

When he picks her up in his arms, cuddling her to him, her cries begin to quieten.

"She's so your girl right now," Kelsea sighs.

"You're my girl too." He leans down kissing her.

It feels like a private moment I'm intruding on as I watch the two of them. Chemistry flows like a river between their bodies. They're whispering something to one another, while he bounces his daughter in his arms. She's beginning to calm down, but I can still see streaks of tears down her cheeks. "Let me try." He takes the bottle from her and slowly coaxes Ella to do her part.

"It's annoying how good you are with her sometimes," Kels huffs.

"Hey." He waits until she looks at him before he hitches his chin, winking. "I'm good with you too."

"That you are." She blushes.

Now it definitely feels like it's too intimate for me. "I'm gonna get out of here. Thank you so much for doing this, Darren." I reach down, giving him a hug. "I'll be in touch about when we need them by."

"No problem, Karsyn." His voice is deeper than I've ever heard it

The way he says it causes me to look at him twice. "See ya." I wave.

"I'll walk you out," Tucker coughs. "Thanks for the advice, Nick."

"Yeah, I mean any time I can say you're a bigger mess than me, it's a win in my book."

Tucker flips him off as he escorts me out, causing me to laugh. We walk out into the night, the sounds loud against the stillness of the sky. "I see I have some competition." He grabs my hand, pulling me toward the driveway.

"Competition?" Now I'm totally confused.

"C'mon, you had to know Darren was hitting on you."

"What?" I giggle. "Are you insane?"

"I could ask the same of you. He's going to go to bed tonight with dreams of you in his head."

"Eww," I laugh, holding my free hand over my mouth. "Don't even joke like that. He's not old enough."

Tucker gives me a look. "Not old enough? He's *just* old enough. You're hot, I mean I'd hit on you too if I were his age."

Biting my lip, I look over at him, smirking. "So you wouldn't hit on me now?"

"I'd definitely hit on you now, too."

We're at my car now, by the driver's side door. "You would?"

He backs me up into it, boxing me in with his arms on the door frame. "I'm trying to," he chuckles. "But you aren't making it very easy."

Glancing up at him, I catch the dark glint of his eyes in the security light they have on their garage. "I made it easy for you before, maybe now I want you to work for it."

"I'll work as hard as I have to." He leans into me. "Do you believe me?"

"I want to."

He lets go of the doorframe, burying his hand in my hair. "You will."

"Wanna come watch a movie with me?" I ask him impulsively. "If you're off-shift and all."

"You okay?" He tilts my head back by pulling slightly on the hair he's grasped.

"I don't want to be alone."

He doesn't look like he totally believes me.

"No, seriously, I just have this feeling that I don't want to be alone. It's okay if you can't," I backpedal.

"Follow me home and let me get some stuff. I need a shower, and clothes to change into. It's late." He looks at his watch. "Going on ten, are you sure?"

"Stay with me." I push my arms around his waist. "Please? I even have the tote bag you gave me in my car. You can totes use it to put your stuff in."

All of a sudden it clicks. "Oh my God, that's why it says totes. It's a tote bag and it's the saying."

"Yes," I laugh. "It's a play on words. I can't believe it took you this long to figure it out." I laugh, harder than I have in a while.

He lets me, but eventually his face gets serious and I start to calm down.

It's then that his lips capture mine. The kiss is measured and totally in control, much like Tucker normally is. "You don't have to ask, just tell me that you want me there."

"I do." I bury my head in his shoulder. "Tonight, I just want you with me."

Tucker

I WATCH in my rearview as Karsyn follows me. I have no idea what's going on with her, but I'm enjoying it. Being the man she wants and needs. For so long she didn't come to me when she had issues. To know she's comfortable enough to tell me she wants me to stay with her? It means everything to me right now.

However, that doesn't mean I'm not going to get to the bottom of what's bothering her. I still know her better than I've ever known a woman. This isn't her normal, and I'll find out what it is.

She's quieter than normal as we get to my house. "I'll just shower at your apartment if that's okay?"

She nods, seemingly wanting to get there. "Sounds good to me."

Again I'm worried about what's happening, but I decide not to broach the subject right now. It might be better to do when we're settled.

I follow her this time, toward her apartment, watching carefully. She's driving slower than normal, and again I wonder what's happened to her in the time we were in the driveway and now.

It's a process, once we get to the parking lot, to get Major and me up to her second-floor one-bedroom, but we do it. I've put my stuff over to the side, locking up my gun, and taking off my shoes when I hear her sharp intake of breath.

"Syn?" Her eyes are wide, face pale, and I'm worried she's going to pass out on me. I hurry over to her, grabbing her wrists. "You've gotta tell me what's going on so I can help you."

Her head shakes, stubborn as all hell.

"No!" My voice is firm. "We stop this trying to save each other the heartache. Tell me what's going on. Let me be the man I want to be in your life."

From her hands a piece of paper drops. Cautiously I let go of her, then bend over and pick it up.

DEAR KARSYN FALLAWAY,

This letter is to inform you of your victim's rights. Inmate in case 08-5555, Clarence Night, has exercised the option for a hearing on his parole. It is recommended you appear at the hearing in Birmingham, AL at the Alabama State Reformatory on May 1st.

It is encouraged you contact your representative on record and arrive at the Reformatory no later than 10 AM on the above date.

If you have any questions, please reach out to your advocate.

Respectfully,

The Alabama State Victim's Notification Services

. . .

"WHY IS HE IN ALABAMA?"

Those are the only words I can get out of my mouth.

She's shivering, so I pull her into my arms. "He was moved after he threatened to kill his cell-mate in Tennessee last year. When we chose to come to Alabama, it was to get as far away from him as I could, and still be in a place where I felt comfortable. By the time we were notified he's here, I'd already started to build a life." She shrugs. "And I refuse to let him ruin anymore of what I have here."

"So who's your advocate or representative?" I ask her, rubbing up and down her back. I can feel the wetness of her tears on my shoulder.

"I don't have one here. The last time I had to appear was in Tennessee."

"We'll get you someone," I assure her, quickly. "There has to be an attorney within the LSERT for situations like this."

"I hope so." She shivers again.

"Is this why you wanted me to stay with you? Did you have a feeling this was going to happen?"

The nod she manages kills me. "It's usually around this time I'm notified, but I honestly thought at some point he'd give up. It doesn't seem like he's ever going to."

"It's a mind game for him." I hold her tightly. "That's all this is."

She's quiet, and when I lean down to kiss her, she clings to me. "Make me forget, Tuck. Please, just make me forget."

It's against my better judgment, but as I pull her to me, I know I'm never going to be able to deny her when she uses that raspy voice of need.

CHAPTER FIFTEEN

Tucker

THE ALARM on my phone wakes me up from one of the worst sleeps I've ever had. Any time Karsyn would move in my arms, I'd wake up to make sure she was alright. I want nothing more than to spend the entire day in bed with her, but unfortunately today is our monthly training with the K-9's. Seeing as how I'm the trainer, I kind of have to be there.

"Do you have to go?"

I roll over so that I'm facing her. From the dark circles under her eyes, I can tell she slept about as well as I did. "Yeah, I have training today."

"Thank you for staying with me last night."

Her face dips down, and I slip my fingers under her chin to lift it back up. "Hey, I'm coming right back when training is over."

"You don't have to."

"I want to." I lean down, kissing her on the forehead. "I want to hear all about what you're going to have to do. Even though I've been in this profession for as long as I have, I honestly have no idea what any of this means for you. I want to be there, help you with this."

"That's sweet." She snuggles back into me.

Sweet isn't the right word, and immediately I want to warn her I feel anything but sweet. I want to rage, bitch at the injustice of it all, and promise her she's never going to get hurt again. Realistically I know none of that is true. She could be hurt crossing the road. And that's the worst part of the situation. Both of us can do everything right, and we might still end up fucked.

"Thank you, Tucker. I know this scared you away before, but I love you. I never stopped loving you when you pushed me away. I was still mad and hurt for a long time, but I couldn't turn off the feelings every time I'd see you drive by my apartment or send me flowers. You showed me how you felt when you made sure I was home safe, even if it was from a distance. I loved you then. Love you now. I'll love you forever. I'm sorry if it scares you, or doesn't fit into your plans, but I'm not hiding how I feel anymore," she whispers, pushing her head into my shoulder.

This is it, my moment to redeem myself. I swore I would if I ever got the chance. Reaching down, I grab her chin between my fingers, tilting it up so those clear eyes of hers are right there for me to see. "I'm scared to death, Karsyn. Scared. To. Death. Because right now I'm not sure if I can keep you safe or not, because I'm about to lay it all on the line. Somehow you got under my skin last year, and I wasn't prepared for it, not even slightly. When you told me you loved me, it blew up my world. That wasn't what I was looking for."

"I know," she interrupts me. "I'm sorry."

Pressing my finger to her lips, I stop her from talking. "Never be sorry about how you feel. That's what I've learned this year, without you in my life."

It takes me a minute to pull my shit together, but I manage because she deserves this. If anyone deserves me putting my guard down, it's Karsyn.

"I'm looking for it now. I want to be the person you come to when you get letters like you just did. If you have someone fucking with you? I'm the person you come to, to take care of it. You're horny, I'm your guy."

She laughs, and I can't help but smile.

"But this guy has grown up." I frame her face with my hands. "Because I also want to be the guy who has your heart, who has those soft looks you give me when you don't think I'm looking. If you need someone to hold you, I'll do it. Want someone to watch TV with you while my dog lays beside you instead of me? I'm there, babe," I lean in, brushing my lips against hers. She closes her eyes, smiling when I pull back slightly. "Because I love you too," I whisper.

She gasps loudly, her eyes flying open. "Tucker?"

"God's honest." I tilt her toward me again. "I've loved you a long time, Karsyn, I just didn't want to admit it. Didn't want to give that kind of power to anyone else. It's a me thing, never a you thing, but I'm mature enough now to realize it was the wrong thing. I should have told you a year ago how I felt, shouldn't have hid anything from you. I'm sorry."

"It's okay." She kisses me, tears streaming down her face. I taste the saltiness, promising myself this is the last time she'll cry because of me.

"It's not okay, but I promise right here, right now to be better for you."

"You're the best." She shakes her head.

I grin. "If love means you'll overlook all my faults, then we'll go with it."

She grins back at me. "Same, Tucker, same."

Another alarm goes off, telling me I have to be at work soon. Groaning, I let go of her. "I have to go."

"Of course." She moves away from me.

My arm tightens around her waist, not letting her get too far away. "Am I coming back here?"

"Yes, actually." She bites her lip. "Do you mind if I go with you? I really don't want to be by myself. I understand if I can't."

"Sure, it'll probably be boring for you, but I'd love to have you if you want to come."

Her eyes are bright again. This time with excitement. "I'll be ready in a few minutes."

"DO IT AGAIN, RANSOM." I have them running through the obstacle course, and Rambo hesitated a little longer than I would like jumping over a fence. Sometimes that means the difference in a suspect getting away and not getting away.

Ransom nods, takes a knee, and talks to Rambo. I get the feeling it's like a dad having a discussion with a child he's disappointed in.

"We're ready," he says as he gets back up.

They go to the beginning of the obstacle course, and while Rambo had been a little slow to begin with, he's sharp this time, doesn't even hesitate at the fence.

"Good job." I clap for them, while Major whines his approval. Using my finger, I motion for the officer from Birmingham to go.

Ransom comes over to where I'm standing, Rambo with him. "Sorry." The apology is totally unnecessary but I do appreciate it.

"No big deal, some days we're just off."

"Keegan's been waking up at four a.m. ready to play the last few weeks, and you know who his favorite playmate is."

I chuckle, looking down at Rambo. He's snoozing next to Ransom. "Poor guy, he's exhausted."

"He is, I didn't even realize what was happening until a few days ago. We're working on how to keep him out of Keegan's room, but he's figured out how to open the door."

"Sounds like you'll be better off figuring out how to get Keegan to sleep through the night."

"Not so easy, asshole. Kids have minds of their own. He's stubborn as fuck too."

"Just like someone else I know," I chuckle.

He groans. "You're not helping the situation."

"You two are done, go ahead and get out of here. I'm gonna release everyone else after this last guy runs. No sense in missing more time with your family. Might be why Keegan's waking up. You know, to spend time with his favorite playmate."

Ransom gives me a look. "Never fuckin' thought of that. You might be right."

"Which is exactly why we need to raise enough money to get a few new dogs."

"Any news on that?"

"I'm meeting with the city council tomorrow to make sure we're okay with the meet and greet. The Captain's okay, but we'll need to shut down a portion of the street in front of the park to have enough room, and that requires the council."

"You may need to make eyes at a few of them."

"Duuddde." I give him a side-eye. "She hits on me every time."

"But you're bringing Karsyn to our events." He points to where Karsyn and Major sit underneath a tree.

"Yeah, so she should just give it up. We're doing good."

He claps me on the back. "Happy for ya, Tuck."

When I glance over at Karsyn, she looks up, our eyes meeting. She smiles so brightly it makes me feel like I've done something amazing. Returning it makes my stomach tingle. "Happy for me too, now get outta here."

The quicker everyone leaves, the quicker I can leave. I don't know about Karsyn, but I'm tired as fuck.

"DO YOU HAVE FAVORITES?" Karsyn asks as we drive back to her apartment. It's been a long day, we're both a little red, and the air conditioner is cranked. I hate how Alabama tends to go from cold to hot as hell in the manner of a week. There is no in-between.

"Favorites?" I'm not quite sure what she's asking.

"You know favorite dogs and handlers?"

"I shouldn't." I grin.

"But do you," she presses.

I wouldn't tell this to just anybody, but she's everything to me. "I don't like the Birmingham guys that much. They think they're better than us because they have a bigger department than we do. Honestly though, they aren't part of the LSERT, so they can suck a dick."

She chokes on her water. "Tuck."

"What? It's the truth. If they knew how to work as a fuckin' team, we'd all be unstoppable. Instead they want to compare. What the fuck ever. There's no way we can compare. They have a bigger department than we do, yet we cover more area because we take care of all the small towns."

"Sorry I asked." She gives me a look.

"What? It's all true."

"I'm sure it is."

"Don't placate me, woman. I know what I know." In the back, Major barks. "See, he agrees."

CHAPTER SIXTEEN

Karsyn

"I CAN'T TELL you how excited I am to have a night out with you two." Stelle claps her hands together as we grab a table at El Chico.

"Same," Kels laughs. "I feel like I haven't been out for a night of fun in a long time, and Tucker offering to drive us home? So fucking sweet. It means I'm free to drink my weight in margaritas."

"I think we're all pretty excited about that." I grin as our waiter comes over.

Stelle takes the lead. "I'm gonna need a pitcher on the rocks, my good man. As well as some chips and queso. Keep it all coming. Mama's having a night out."

"With pleasure, my friend," he laughs as he gets a good look at us.

"It's almost like he knows he's going to get an amazingly good tip." Stella looks around at us. "Like I'm prepared to give him a hundred bucks as long as I don't have to worry about anyone but myself."

"Amen." Kelsea holds her hand up for a high-five.

I look at the two of them, so thankful to be out together. It's been too long since the three of us had a girls night out. Understandable though, they're both mothers now, and I've been dealing with Tucker and the hearing.

The food and drinks are dropped off. We immediately begin digging into both, sharing stories we haven't been able to share in a while.

"D walked in on us screwing around." Kels covers her face with her hands. "I mean we weren't full-on fucking," she giggles.

"Well thank God for that." Stella gives her a smirk.

"But I did have his dick down my throat, and I was on my knees in front of him."

"Oh my God," I giggle. "That's awful."

"Nick tried to make me feel better by saying D's probably been wondering about this stuff for a while, but trust me, that didn't make me feel better."

"Thank God we don't have an older kid in the house." Stella pours herself another drink. "I had a fucking shit fit when Ransom and I tried to get back on the horse after I had Keegan."

"Why?" I'm listening with all ears. Anything that happens to Stella is worth listening to.

"So we're going at it, and I mean it's feeling good. Like feeling good for the first time. I'm on top, grinding against him, he's got his hands planted on my ass, he leans up with those strong ab muscles of his to take my nipple in his mouth, and that's when I feel it."

Kelsea is groaning.

I'm lost. "Feel what?"

"My milk." Stella puts her face in her hands. "It leaks and goes everywhere. I was so embarrassed."

"That's happened to me, too." Kelsea shakes her head. "Talk about killing the mood."

"Yes!" Stella agrees. "I didn't let him touch me for like three weeks after that."

I'm quiet thinking about what's going on in my life.

"So what do you have to share with us?" Kels asks, taking another drink of her margarita.

No time like the present. "I was kidnapped as a kid and my kidnapper is up for parole. I have to go speak before the board."

They look at me, their mouths wide open.

"What the actual fuck?" Stella sits up straighter. "Why didn't you tell us while we were sharing our stupid tales of sex."

"Yeah." Kels leans in. "This is real-life shit.

I squirm in my chair. "Because it is real-life shit, and because I don't like to talk about it."

"Too bad." Stella glares at me. "Spill."

As I start speaking, I realize I finally trust my friends enough to be honest, and it's the best feeling in the world.

Tucker

N: **Your girlfriend has taken my wife for the night.**

R: Mine too, and I'm off-work. Obviously since you're out there.

These two are always bitching to me about something.

T: Cry a little more for me. They wanted to have a Girls Night Out. You know I'm going to pick them all up. You should be thanking me. They'll probably be drunk and ready to go when I get them home.

N: Yeah, ready to go to sleep.

R: Same. Meanwhile I'm stuck watching Mickey Mouse Playhouse hoping like hell Keegan realizes it's time to go to bed sometime soon.

T: Bitch a little more for me.

R: Oh, I can.

N: Me too! Ella puked on me earlier, and I'm not talking a little bit of spit-up. She went full-on exorcist style. Her head legit spun around. I sympathy-puked. I haven't done that since Kels was pregnant.

I'm laughing as I work on my reports for the night.

T: There's no way that sweet little girl is a demon.

N: Man, you didn't see what came out of her body.

R: You keep that over at your own house, bro. This is what I'm dealing with.

He sends me a picture of Keegan sitting against Rambo, the two of them watching TV.

T: Looks like your dog is doing the watching, and you're just spending your time bitching.

R: Screw you, man.

T: You'll be thanking me when your wife's have had a nice, relaxing time and are ready to have some fun with you when they get home.

N: We'll see. Right now Kels refuses to do anything with me after D caught us.

R: Oh shit!

N: Yeah, this house is a nookie-free zone.

A new text comes through. It's a picture of the three girls, smiles on their faces.

K: We're ready to go, Tuck. If you're ready to come get us.

T: Be right there, babe.

I switch back over to the group text.

T: Look alive boys, the ladies requested a pick up.

R: Okay, time to get this baby down!

N: Right? Just told D I have to take a shower.

T: What? No thank you?

R: Fuck you.

N: I'm nicer, we'll see how the rest of the night goes. IF you're owed a thank you, you'll get it tomorrow.

I chuckle, thinking about how different their lives are from when I met them. I don't think any of us would have it any other way.

CHAPTER SEVENTEEN

Karsyn

"THANKS FOR COMING WITH ME TODAY." I get into Tucker's truck, smoothing my skirt down.

I took a half-day at work, because I'm going to go meet with my new victim advocate. Smarter than I ever gave him credit for, Tucker's idea of looking through the LSERT got me an attorney who took my case as soon as she heard my problem. Today, I'm going to meet Shelby Bruce.

"No problem." He reaches over, grabbing my hand with his. "You know I'll be with you every step of the way."

"I know, but I'm still nervous." I worry with my hair, twirling a strand of it around my finger.

"It's understandable. What are you most nervous about?"

How do I explain to him that I think I'm going to have to relive what happened to me this time? "Telling my story. Previously, the people in Tennessee knew what happened. They remembered it vividly, I never truly had to tell the story. Here, I think most people aren't going to know, and I'll have to explain in great detail. Then what if they don't believe me?"

"They're going to believe you."

"It seems like more often than not, the people in jail have more rights than the victim." I swallow roughly. "I know as an officer of the law, it hurts you to hear that, but it's true."

"No, I mean, I get you. Sometimes it does seem like that, but I get the feeling whatever you're going to talk about, is going to resonate with whoever hears it. You're so good at conveying your feelings."

"Not about this." I run my free hand along my skirt again. "It's super hard to talk about this, even when I'm prepared. It completely changed my life."

"Look I'm not going to pretend that I understand, even a little bit, of what you've gone through. What I can tell you with confidence is that you're an amazing woman who speaks eloquently and with a sureness of herself that not many people have these days. You've got this, although I'm surprised your parents aren't here."

The words bring tears to my eyes. "I hope I do, and I asked them not to come. They still don't know everything that happened to me, and I just don't want to break their hearts. They've been through enough."

"They would still be there for you if you let them, Syn. I know you do, because I believe in you, and if I have to do it for the both of us, then that's fine. I will."

Who is this Tucker? He's the one I wanted in the beginning, and he'd disappointed me so much when I'd opened my heart to him. This is the man I've wanted the entire time, the one I need so much right now. "I can't even begin to tell you how much I appreciate you."

"This is what a man who loves the woman beside him does, Karsyn, and I'm sorry I made you question that about us."

I don't say anything this time, because I can't. There's nothing to say that won't make me cry like a baby. Instead, I hold his hand tighter, looking out the window as we travel into downtown Laurel Springs.

"Where did she say she was?" he asks as he enters the downtown square.

"In the old Fischer Building." I point to a sign reading *Shelby Bruce Attorney At Law.*

He gets a parking spot at the front of the building, walking over to help me out.

"We can make a run for it," he jokes, causing me to grin.

Instead I grab him around the neck, pulling him into me, hugging tightly. "We could, but then he would win."

"And we can't let him win," he finishes.

"We can't."

He helps me down, and with our fingers entwined we walk up to her office, entering together.

There are moments of your life when you know something is going to change, a feeling of not only dread but of knowing you don't have control of a situation. That feeling engulfs me as I walk into this office. At the same time, I get an overwhelming sense that this is where I'm supposed to be.

Before we can sit down, a woman comes out of the office. She's what I would call movie-star gorgeous. Long blonde-hair, tall, tan, her makeup perfect, her nails manicured. She gives me a welcoming smile, holding out her hand. "Karsyn? I'm Shelby."

"Nice to meet you." I shake it gratefully. She gives off an air of knowing exactly what to do in every situation and getting exactly what she wants, when she wants it. "This is Tucker, my boyfriend."

She shakes his hand just like she did with mine, escorting us into her office. When we get in there, I take a moment to look at the plaques. She graduated from the University of Mississippi School of Law two years ago, and judging by the pictures, she has a family who adores her.

"It's good to have the two of you here today. Since I've never represented you before, and this is the first time we've met, I'll tell you a little about myself. I graduated in the top five percent of my class. For the past two years I worked as a public defender for the state of Mississippi. When my contract was over, I landed here, opening this law firm. I've only been in town a few months, but I got connected with the LSERT a few weeks ago, and you're the first case I've taken through LSERT. Knowing you're a member just like me makes me excited to be helping you out."

"Thank you for helping." Tucker situates himself next to me, putting his arm behind my chair.

"Now why don't you tell me a little about your case? I've pulled some articles, but I haven't been able to get fully acquainted. I will before his parole hearing, make no mistake about that."

"I understand." I lean forward, rubbing my neck. "You just found out about this yesterday. Thank you for taking me on so quickly."

"I'm excited to be in a community that helps each other." She smiles brightly.

There's a notepad in front of her, pen poised to take down what I'm about to tell her. Slowly I recount the story I previously told Tucker.

"Wow." She shakes her head. "And they're contemplating giving him parole? This is exactly why I had to leave the public defender's office. Now I know this may be a little harder, but I need to know what happened when you were with him? There are two days unaccounted for."

Those days I was in his car, traveling the state of Tennessee, trying to evade police. Those forty-eight hours are ingrained in my brain. Sometimes they play like a movie that I'm not actually a part of. Other times they roll through like a timeline of my life.

"Did he threaten you?" she asks carefully.

"Many times. The few times I defied him, he said he would kill me. When I told him to go ahead, because I knew I'd meet God, he threatened to rape me." This is harder for me to talk about. The part I didn't tell Tucker. "Said he'd ruin me for other men. He described in great detail about how he'd mutilate my body, and take my virginity. It was those words that kept me doing what he asked of me," I admit, my throat getting clogged. "You have to understand as a girl my age, that was terrifying."

"It would be terrifying to anyone, no matter the age, Karsyn." She shakes her head as she takes a few more notes. "Anything else I need to know?"

"He's tattooed," I whisper.

This is important, because it proves he exposed himself to me. It proves I saw more than I ever wanted to.

"Where?" Her pen stays poised on the paper.

"His penis." I lick my suddenly dry lips. "You can't read it unless it's erect, though."

Her lips are thin as I finish my sentence.

"What does it say?"

The phrase will always be there at the back of my mind, even if I want to forget it. It's one of those memories I'll never be able to completely let go of.

"Poison."

TUCKER and I are quiet as we sit in his truck after leaving the appointment. Both of us are lost in our respective thoughts, but there's one thing I need to know.

"Do you think of me any differently?"

"What the fuck, Karsyn? What makes you think I think of you differently?"

"You're quiet, and you have been since we left Shelby's office."

He pulls the truck over to the side of the road, turning to face me after he puts his hazards on.

"I'm fucking pissed, Karsyn. Not because of anything you did, but because of everything he did. You were a kid, someone who was scared to death, and he did whatever it took to assert himself over you. I can only imagine how long it took you to overcome issues with looking at guys and their dicks."

I flinch, not because of what he said, but because it's true. "I was a virgin until my senior year of college. I never had good sex until you."

"Never?" He raises his eyebrows.

"I never let myself go until you. Didn't have an orgasm until you. There was something about the way you made me feel protected. I knew you wouldn't hurt me." I shrug. I can't explain exactly the way he makes me feel, and I feel like I would come up empty if I did."

He grabs my hands. "I will always make sure you're protected, Karsyn. Nobody will hurt you on my fuckin' watch. It's me or them."

And I know without a doubt he's telling me the truth.

CHAPTER EIGHTEEN

Tucker

NORMALLY I DON'T ATTACK my workouts with the ferociousness I'm attacking this one with today. Most of the guys I typically get in the department gym with will tell you I'm level. I jog at a consistent pace; I don't go fast then slow, I don't lift heavy then light. Always level-headed, always the median. That's me.

Today though? Today all the fucking anger about what happened to Karsyn is coming out. I'm looking to completely exhaust my body, because I don't want to have another night of tossing and turning, trying to get what I learned happen to her out of my head. I'd thought I'd been prepared to hear, being the tough guy I am, seeing what I've seen.

None of that prepared me for how I felt when I listened to what had happened to her. As a cop, I can definitely separate myself from the victims I help every day. This situation taught me I can't separate myself from Karsyn.

"You may wanna slow it down," Ransom says as he starts on the treadmill next to me. "You're gonna stomp a hole in the machine."

It's then I realize I'm pounding harder than I meant to. So far in my zone I hadn't even heard the loud noises I was making. "Sorry." I put my feet on either side of the treadmill and turn it to a slower speed. "Just trying to work out some frustration."

I have to give it to Ransom, he doesn't crack a joke, which I know is hard for him. He's very much a jokester in almost every situation. "Anything you want to talk about?"

"Not right now." I grab my water bottle, draining it dry. "No disrespect to you, but I need to wrap my own head around what's going on before I can explain it to anyone else. And honestly it's not my secret to tell."

"Just know I'm here if you need me."

I nod as I do my cool-down. It means a lot to know he's there, but it also reminds me that Karsyn had to suffer with most of this possibly without others to help her. When I'm done, I head to the locker room area, getting ready to go on-shift. Major is laying right where I left him - in front of my locker. "Let me take a shower, and then we can do work."

He barks like he completely understands what I'm saying to him. He gets me in ways I'm not sure many people get me. "Love ya, Major." I reach down rubbing his nose. He barks again, which I take for he loves me too.

WE'VE MADE a few laps around Laurel Springs, but nothing seems to be happening so far tonight, which I'm thankful for. My mind isn't where it should be at all. I'm still angry, upset, and a million other things about what Karsyn's being put through.

My phone chimes with an incoming text.

K: This may be a weird question, but do you mind if I stay at your house tonight? I just, don't want to be at my apartment.

T: No, I want you there, if that's where you want to be. Want to meet me to get the key?

K: If it's not a problem, I know you're at work.

T: Nothing's ever a problem for you.

K: Thanks, Tuck.

T: Let me know when you're ready to leave and I'll tell you where I am.

K: I'm ready now.

For some reason that makes me laugh, and it's welcome, because I feel like there's been precious little to laugh at since she told me what the hell is going on with her.

T: I'm taking speed out at the bottoms.

K: Setting up a trap aren't ya, Officer Williams?

T: It got me you, didn't it?

K: LOL! Busted! I'll be there in a few.

Mentioning it, reminds me of the day I pulled Karsyn over. I'd seen her in town a few times. Laurel Springs is small enough that you tend to see the same people over and over again. But that day, when I pulled over the sleek, black, Charger, I had no idea there was a woman behind the wheel, and I obviously didn't know how beautiful she was.

"Is there a problem, officer?"

I do my best to keep the irritation off my face, why does everyone ask that question first? If there wasn't a problem, would I be stopping them?

"You were going sixty-five back there. It's a fifty mile an hour posted limit. License and registration, please."

It's then I see her, the eyes, the hair, the innocent freaking face.

She reaches over into her glovebox. "I'm so sorry, I'm new in town. Well actually I've lived in the area for the past few years, but I just moved into Laurel Springs about six months ago, and I'm learning the layout. Graduated, moved out, and became an adult and all," she laughs as she explains, handing me what I've asked for.

"Well, Ms. Fallaway?" I question, waiting for her to correct me. I don't see a wedding ring, but these days that doesn't mean much.

"Yes," she confirms.

"I'd love to let you go with a warning, but fifteen miles is too much for me to do that. If everything comes back okay, you'll be getting a ticket, but I'll knock it down for you."

There are tears in her eyes, but I'm not sure if that's because she's trying to get me to go easier on her, or if that's how she reacts to aspects of her life. She nods, stiffening her lip, and I know without a doubt this girl is strong. She's slightly pissed, I can tell by the way her jaw tightens, and the fire that accompanies those tears in her eyes.

Glancing at my watch, I know she'll be here sooner rather than later. I miss her, even though it's only been a few hours. Letting her into my life has been more encompassing than I ever imagined it would be.

Major barks slightly, alerting me that someone is pulling in behind me. When I look back, I see Karsyn, waving as she gets out. Just seeing her causes me to grin.

"Hey," I greet her as I get out of the driver's seat.

"Hey." She grins back, meeting me in the middle.

Our arms go around each other, clasping in a hug that warms me to my soul. I didn't know how much I needed this hug until she was here in my arms. She makes a small sound in her throat, and immediately my mind goes to dirtier places than where we are right now.

Pulling back slightly, I look down, grab her chin in my fingers and lean in for a kiss. It's one of barely-leashed passion with a touch of possession. Fuck if I'm on the side of the road wearing my uniform. This woman does it for me, and I want not only her, but anyone else who cares to be watching, to know it.

We separate slowly. I open my eyes just as slowly, watching as she runs her tongue along her lips. Her eyes and she stares at me, smirking. "You taste good, Tuck."

A groan works its way past my throat. "You think so?"

"I do."

I move her around to the back of my SUV, leaning her up against the bumper. Crowding into her personal space, I let her scent and the aura that is Karsyn Fallaway wash all over me. "Wish I didn't have to work the rest of the night." I grab a piece of her hair, twirling it around my finger before letting it fall.

"I wish you didn't either, but at least your bed smells like you." She widens her legs slightly, letting me rest closer in between those thighs of hers.

"Then when I go to sleep, it'll smell like you." I toss my

head back, rolling my eyes skyward. "Working second shift while you work first sucks."

She giggles, running her hands along my chest, before coming to meet in the middle and moving down to the waistband of my pants. "Makes the heart grow fonder," she teases.

"Makes me hornier," I throw back at her.

As we stand there, staring at one another, each daring the other to make a move, a car speeds by. She clears her throat. "Maybe you should get back to work."

"Yeah," I sigh. "Maybe I should."

Grabbing her hand, I walk her to the front of the SUV, before reaching in to get my keys. It takes a few seconds, but I get my house key off the ring. "Here ya go." I hold it up to her.

She palms it. "Thanks, I'll leave it on your counter." She stands up on her tiptoes, kissing me softly.

Wrapping my arm around her, I hold her to me. "Nah, I got another one hidden at the house. You keep this one."

"Tuck?"

Surprise colors her face red, her eyes dart back and forth, probably wondering if I'm being serious or not.

"It's time, Karsyn. You keep it. Whenever you feel the need to be close to me, don't hesitate to use it."

Tears pool, and she does her best to blink them away. "You're special, more special than you'll ever realize."

Gently, I grab her around the neck, tilting her face up to mine. "You're the only person in my adult life who's made me want to be special, Karsyn. Don't forget that. It's you and only you. We may have fucked this up before, but I promise you, we're not fuckin' it up again.

She smiles widely. "I'll see you when you get home."

As she walks off, I find myself calling out to her. "Be safe."

"You too, officer."

With a laugh and a wave, I watch her drive away. The smile doesn't leave my face and I don't think it will for the rest of the night.

CHAPTER NINETEEN

Karsyn

FLOORED IS AN UNDERSTATEMENT, I never expected Tucker to give me a key to his house. Parking in his driveway, I feel a warmth in my heart I haven't felt in a long time. I'm trying to temper my expectations, but it's hard when Tucker keeps blowing them out of the water.

My cell buzzes in the cup holder. Reaching over, I grab it out, smiling as I see a message from the man on my mind.

T: The code to turn the alarm off is 6701.

K: Thank you! I didn't even think about that.

T: The last thing you need is the alarm company calling the cops because you're in a cop's house without the alarm code.

K: True! Unless that means you're gonna be the one cuffing and strip searching me! ::wink::

Grabbing up all my stuff, I get out of the car, shutting the driver's side door with my hip. It's odd, turning this key and walking into his lair. It's like the culmination of a dream I knew I had, but didn't want to admit.

For the first time, I allow myself to look around, to really gaze into the man I've loved for longer than I care to admit. Without his watchful eye, I take a few moments, looking at the pictures on his shelving unit. A grin breaks across my face as I see Major front and center. There's Ransom and a couple of the other men he's trained, Rambo and Major together, and the group of Laurel Springs officers. There's an older couple that has to be his parents. He doesn't talk about them much. There's a picture of him in his military uniform. What stares back at me is a younger man, without the facial hair, his lips flattened into a firm line. Behind him the American Flag is superimposed. He must have been in his early twenties. I wonder what he was like back then. Would he and I have gotten along?

Maybe it's something I should ask him. How he's changed.

The air kicks on, scaring the hell out of me. I've snooped enough, and it's like the house knew it.

DEEP in my subconscious I can hear my alarm going off. Typically I let it go for longer than I should, but I'm at Tucker's, I remind myself. He probably just went to sleep a few hours ago, and he definitely needs his sleep more than I do.

Grabbing the phone, I stab my finger at it to shut the alarm off. That's when I realize I'm wrapped in strong, firm, masculine arms. With a sigh, I sink deeper into them, wondering how in the world this is my life.

"Morning," his scratchy voice whispers in my ear.

"I didn't mean to wake you up," I whisper.

"S'okay, I'm a light sleeper. It comes from years of getting woken up to go run a mission or to be at a crime scene. I'll go back to sleep soon." He kisses the side of my temple.

"I'll grab my stuff and go get ready in the other bathroom." The promise is in my voice, but I can't seem to pull myself out of his arms.

"No, I like knowing you're getting ready in here while I'm sleeping."

The softly admitted secret is enough to make my heart pound faster. Like who knew this could be Tucker? As hard as we fought against one another, who knew this could be us?

"If Major acts like he needs to go out, can you let him? He'll let you know when he's ready to come back in by scratching on the doorframe. He's really good about it."

"Yeah." I grin. "No problem." I lean over, kissing him on the forehead. "Go back to sleep."

He drifts off and the grin is stuck there, him giving me something to do for Major is like giving me something to do to watch his child. It's a supreme act of trust and I'm floored by it.

"YOU SPENT the night at Tucker's?" Kels squeals as we're getting ready to open the clinic.

"I did."

I still haven't been able to wipe the smile off my face. My sleep last night was better than anything I've had in years. I don't know if it was because I was in his bed, or it's because I felt so safe in his space. Waking up this morning was the best.

"He even asked me to take care of Major for him."

"Girl." She looks at me, her eyes wide, smirk tilted up. "That's progress. You know as well as I do those dogs should just be their kids."

"I know, and I'm almost giddy at being trusted with him. Maybe this is a turning point in our relationship."

"Do you think he's changed?"

It's hard to be objective because that's my biggest hope, that he's willing to allow me in his life. I don't want to get all fucked up about it and be like one of those women who think just because we had sex he loves me, but there's something different here this time. The way he looks at me is softer, the way he holds me is stronger, and I swear sometimes it's like he's touching my soul when we're together.

"Yeah, I think he has. I think he's willing to look at things from my perspective now, and just maybe I've wormed myself into his heart, ya know? We're definitely closer than we were."

"I'm so happy to hear that." She reaches over, giving me a hug. "I want everyone to have a love like mine and Nick's. He cautions me though, all the time, that I don't need to get involved."

"Trust me, I know," I laugh. "It's hard, but I think this time, Tucker and I have figured some things out. We'll see, but he seems to be opening himself up to me in ways he's never opened up before. The thing hanging over my head this time isn't Tucker." I frown as I think about the parole hearing.

She immediately stops what she's doing, glancing over at me. "What's going on?"

"My kidnapper," I still hate saying that phrase, giving him the power over me he's assumed over the years, "is up for parole. I'm going to go before the board and speak. I'm nervous," I admit.

"Oh Karsyn." She gathers me up in a hug. "When did you find out about this?"

"A few days ago. Tucker went with me to meet my new victims advocate, and I think I have a very good shot at keeping him in prison," I trail off. "It's just stressful, I hate talking about what he did to me, I resent having to go back through it, and I just don't understand why I have to honestly be the person who holds him accountable."

"It sucks, it seems like the perpetrators sometimes have more rights than the victims."

"That's exactly what I said to Tucker, and I felt awful saying that because he works so hard to put the bad guys away."

Kels is quiet now. "Is everything okay with you?"

She clears her throat. "Yeah, it's just..." she trails off.

"Just what?" I prompt her.

"This is so fucking embarrassing," she giggles.

"Hello." I look around at where we are. "We work in the medical field. We've not only seen embarrassing situations with other people, but with ourselves too. You know you can tell me anything."

"Okay," she sighs. "Since we had Ella, Nick and I haven't, ya know?"

I'm not understanding what she's saying. "No, I don't know. You'll have to spell it out for me."

"We haven't had any time alone. Either Ella needs to be taken care of, or D needs something. Mom and Dad are always watching Caleb and Ruby's kids when I want to ask them to watch ours, and I feel awful giving them four kids, one basically a newborn to watch. Caleb and Ruby don't get enough time as is, Stelle and Ransom have one of their own, and the three times we tried to ask Whitney and Ryan to watch Ella, they were already watching Keegan. Our timing is just totally off." She finishes the rest of her story, pressing the words out in a rush.

"You need someone to watch your kids so that you and your husband can have uninterrupted sexy time? Am I understanding this?" I need to make sure I get where she's coming from.

"Yes." She buries her face in her hands. "I told you it was embarrassing."

I start giggling until it turns into a full-body laugh.

"This isn't funny." She crosses her arms over her chest. "I fail to see the humor in the situation."

"It's not that big of a deal." I wipe below my eyes. "I thought you were going to tell me something completely awful."

"Dude it is! We're going on like six months here. Things are getting critical."

I laugh harder again. "I can watch them."

The offer is out before I even think about it.

"Are you sure?" She looks at me with mixed parts hope and uncertainty.

"Yeah, I used to babysit kids when I was younger. It's not that big of a deal. If you need some time alone, I can watch them for the afternoon, evening, whatever you want. I'm probably not good for overnight," I caution.

"We would never ask that." She bites her nail.

I can see the hope in her eyes, the excitement.

"Let me talk to Nick about it, and I'll get back to you?"

"Just let me know what you wanna do, Kels. I'm here for you, just like you're here for me."

"You are." She reaches over, grabbing my hand in hers. "And if you need me when you have to the parole hearing, just let me know."

I nod, trying to ignore the dark cloud hanging so low over my head.

CHAPTER TWENTY

Tucker

"WHAT THE FUCK IS THIS MEETING?" I have a seat next to Ransom.

I was awoken by a phone call saying that every available officer in the area needed to report to the Laurel Springs PD for a mandatory meeting.

"No fuckin' idea," he yawns. "My ass was asleep, I didn't even brush my hair."

Glancing up at him, I see that it's every which way, and Rambo is most definitely asleep at his feet.

"Same." I grin.

"Fuck you, dude, you don't even have to brush your hair."

"I was still woken up, so don't bitch at me like I don't understand your plight."

He rolls his eyes. "Do you have to use such big words?"

"Yes, yes I do."

He flips me off, and right as I'm about to say something

else to him, Mason steps in front of the group. "I'll be giving a briefing in just a few minutes, if everyone could start to settle down and find a seat."

That's his way of letting everyone know we're being too loud and he wants us to shut the fuck up. I'm cracking my back as Nick and Caleb enter the room. I wave them over to sit with us.

"Fuck, man." Nick runs a hand over his face. "I had just gotten Ella down and was about to try and get a few hours when the phone rang."

"Whose watching Ella?" Ransom asks as he looks over at his friend.

"Your Mom," he laughs. "Don't even ask how it came to that, it just did. She's a saint."

"That's my mom, she'll have your kid wired up on sugar in less than an hour. RIP to any sleep you wanted to get today."

"Fuck me." He reaches over, grabbing his bottle of Mountain Dew.

"This all makes me thankful all I have to worry about is a dog."

"Screw you," Ransom mumbles. "I'm sure your day is coming."

For the first time in years I think about what it would be like to have a kid. I've only thought about it once before, with a woman I should never have imagined it with. But with Karsyn? I can see it. She's such a giving person with patience and a real desire to help anyone out that needs it. She and I are a lot alike in that respect. It's one of the things I love most about her.

Still weird to think about love, but at least I'm admitting it now.

Menace whistles, hoping to get everyone to stop moving around.

It takes the room a little under thirty seconds to calm down and pay attention to him, which is the epitome of a good leader.

"First of all, I wanna thank everybody for being here." He nods to a few members of the group. "I know we woke some of y'all up, and for that we're sorry. I think though, after we give you the briefing, you'll be glad we did."

Now I'm sitting up straight, and wondering what the fuck is going on. He's not the type of guy to say things for reaction. If it's important, he makes sure we know it. He wouldn't have gotten all these men out of bed if there wasn't a good reason for it.

"There's been some talk at the federal prison in Birmingham that there's going to be an attempted break."

Shit.

"Do we know who?" I ask immediately. That prison holds some of the worst offenders. Any federal prison is dangerous, but this one? It's housing some bad people.

"No," he confirms. "Which is what makes this even worse."

"How did we find out?" Caleb calls out from where he sits.

"Jailhouse informant," Mason answers immediately. "Most of the time these things are taken with a grain of salt, but this particular informant has been right about two other incidents that have happened recently. If you'll hold all of your questions, I'll tell you what we do know."

The room is slightly buzzing with an undercurrent of unease. All of us know what this means, depending on who gets out, we could have a crime spree, and if that's the case, it's going to take not only the Birmingham officers, but the LSERT will be called in to assist, especially our K-9's.

"What we know is that the plan is for no more than ten to break out, no less than five. The facility is a medium to maximum security prison, but it's one of the oldest in the country, meaning there are weaknesses in its infrastructure that smart enough prisoners could breach. Let's face it. They got nothing but time, so I think we have to take this seriously."

I raise my hand and when Menace nods at me, I ask the question burning in my gut. "Do we know what the plan is?"

"That's where this gets tricky," he explains. "There have been several mentioned. Anything from a secret tunnel to someone faking a medical emergency. We honestly don't know."

And that's the worst part about doing what we do. So many times we only have part of the plan and none of the information we really need to protect the public. That only comes when someone talks, or the plan is already in motion.

"What I'm saying to all of you is that we need to be on high alert. Whatever this is, I don't think it needs to be taken lightly. It's been over a decade since anyone tried to break out of that prison. It's time."

Fear immediately settles deep in my stomach, because that's the prison I'll be going to, to be emotional support for Karsyn. Something doesn't sit well with me about this whole situation, but I keep it inside as we continue to pay attention to Menace. Some of us take notes, but the rest of us, we listen with passive faces, doing our best to rein in our emotions.

"Do we know when this is supposed to happen?" Nick asks. "Like do we have any sort of timeframe?"

"I wish I could give you that." Menace rocks back and

forth on his heels, running his hand along his gray beard. "But I can't. All the info we have is what I've given to you today."

"Which is jack shit," Nick whispers.

A laugh almost works its way past my throat, but this is too serious a situation for that kind of response.

"Well fuck," Caleb sighs as we get done. "That wasn't helpful at all. I hate that we don't even know when we can expect this shit to happen."

"At least we have a heads up." Menace comes to where we're standing, putting a hand on his son's back. "You know me, you know if I didn't think it was credible, I wouldn't have pulled everyone together for this."

"Oh I have no doubt, and trust me when I say this isn't about you, it's about the uncertainty. I fucking hate it."

"We all do," I pipe up. "I'm going down there in the next few days. Not to go into the whole story, but Karsyn knows someone whose up for parole, and she's testifying against them."

Menace's eyebrows draw together. "Are you fuckin' kidding me?"

"I wish I was."

"This shit isn't sitting well with me." He runs a hand through his hair. "Birmingham seems to think it's not as credible as I do, but I've got a really bad feeling about it."

"I do too," I admit. "It's almost like when you're in a forest with no noise, you know more than anything there's something there that can kill you, but you don't know who or what it is until they show themselves."

"Exactly." He shoves his hands in his jeans pockets. "I just need you all to be ready, it's the only reason I called this meeting. There's a bigger LSERT meeting happening tomorrow, which I don't expect you all to attend. I wanted to be able to talk to y'all separately."

"I'm keeping Karsyn away from that meeting," I warn him. "She's already nervous enough about what's happening. I don't need her to be scared of this too."

"I think that's a good idea," they all agree with me.

"Just stay alert," Menace reminds us. "If we plan for the worst, and it doesn't happen then we're over-prepared and I'd rather be over-prepared than under. When you're under, people get hurt and I refuse for that shit to happen under my watch.

As we all get ready to leave, I'm doing my best to think about how I'm going to approach this situation with Karsyn. She needs to know, but she doesn't need to find out in the middle of a LSERT meeting. As I'm rolling scenarios around in my mind, my phone buzzes, and I reach down, seeing her smiling face. There's a text message, immediately I open it, and wonder just what in the fuck I got myself into.

K: So how are you with kids?

T: Ummm is there something you need to tell me?

K: Just that we're watching Kels and Nick's kids for a few hours tonight. You're off right?

T: I am, but why are we watching their kids?

K: So they can have uninterrupted sexy time.

T: Oh really?

This right here is going to make perfect ammunition to annoy the shit out of Nick, and even if she hadn't already offered up my services, I would with a smile on my face.

K: Be nice, Tucker.

T: Babe...I'm always nice!

CHAPTER TWENTY-ONE

Karsyn

"THANK YOU AGAIN!"

"You don't have to thank me," I remind Kelsea one more time. "It's really not that big of a deal. If you want to thank someone, thank Tucker for letting us use his house." I look back at Tucker who has the biggest smile on his face.

"Thank you, Tucker." She hugs him. "I appreciate it, so much."

"No problem." He smiles wider, and I just know he's planning to do something.

"Go, get home to your hubby." I push her toward the door. "Ella's asleep and D is playing with Major. Get out while you can."

"We'll be back to pick them up." She worries her lip in between her teeth.

"I didn't think you'd just leave them here," Tucker deadpans. "I'm down to watch them for a few hours, but I'm too selfish to be a parent right now."

Kelsea's smile disappears from her face. "Oh no, that's not what I meant."

"He's joking, Kels. Go!"

This time I do push her out of the door, locking it when I finally get her past the threshold. "What are you doing?" I look at him closely.

"Me?" He points to his chest. "What makes you think I'm doing something?"

"I know you, and I just have a feeling."

He comes over to me, wrapping an arm around my neck, steering me to the kitchen where we've left Ella sleeping in her carrier. "I didn't steal Nick's phone and set an alarm to go off every hour for the next four hours. Not me."

"Tucker! He's going to kill you."

"He can try, but I'm older and wiser."

"That's so mean, who knows when the last time was they had sex with no interruptions."

"He'll get pissed, throw the phone, and it won't matter. Trust me."

We get to the kitchen and I go over to check on Ella. She's still snoozing in her carrier, I don't want to wake her up, so I sit her in the middle of the kitchen table so I can keep an eye on her.

"What are you planning on feeding this kid for dinner?" Tucker asks as he looks out the window, watching Major and Darren playing.

It strikes me in this instant that Tucker and I have never really sat down to a meal together that we cooked. There are so many things we've done, I sometimes forget about the things we haven't done.

"I went to the grocery on the way over here." I point to the Kroger bag on the counter. "I got stuff to make pizza with, and some ice cream that I've already put in the freezer."

"Ice cream?" His interest is piqued. "I got a fuckin' big sweet tooth. What kind did you get?"

"How did I not know this about you?" I laugh as I go over to pull the cookies and cream out of the freezer.

"There's a lot we don't know, that we need to get to know." He looks in, grinning. "Not my favorite, but it'll do."

"Let's start with what is your favorite."

"I'm a simple man." He rubs his hand over his stomach. "Chocolate with chocolate syrup."

"Chocolate on chocolate, I should have guessed when you told me you had a sweet tooth."

"What's yours?" He turns the question around on me.

"Chocolate and strawberry mixed together with strawberries and chocolate syrup. Put a little whipped cream on top of it, and that's my jam."

"You like a whole-ass sundae."

"I mean, it is what it is." I turn from him, closing the door to the freezer. "My tastes are extravagant sometimes."

"Oh really?" He turns me back around to face him.

"Really." I tilt my head up to him.

He leans in, grabbing my lips with his. It's tame compared to the way we've kissed in the past. When he pulls back, he licks those lips of his. "As extravagant as I figured."

Pinching his stomach, I giggle. "Don't be a smartass."

"You know you love it." He wraps me up in his arms.

Tilting my head down so that I can tuck in under his chin, I wrap my arms around his waist. "I do," I whisper.

"I do too," he whispers back, and this right here is one of the best moments I can remember us ever sharing.

It's broken apart as Darren and Major come barreling into the kitchen.

"You hungry?" I ask him as he has a seat at the table, breathing heavily.

"Starving! Major made me run all over the place. What are you feeding me?"

"I have it on good authority you like pizza?"

He makes a noise. "Pizza is my favorite!"

Major barks loudly, causing everyone to shush him when Ella stirs.

"I get it," I laugh. "You're hungry too."

He comes over to me, nudging me with his nose. I tap against my thighs and he quickly stands on his hind legs, I give him a scratch behind his ears. His tail wags wildly behind him. "Feels good doesn't it." I rub harder.

"C'mon, Bud, time to eat." Tucker puts his food down, shaking it.

It takes Major a few moments to hop down and go over to his food. "When you're around and he's not on duty, it's like he listens to you better."

"He knows who lets him sleep in the bed when you're not watching."

"You two team up on me and it's not fair."

I give him a smile. "At least somebody's on my side."

"Babe, everybody is on your side."

"WHAT DO YOU LIKE ON YOURS?" I ask Darren as the two of us stand in front of our two pans of pizza dough. "I have pepperoni, some veggies, pineapple, beef." I rifle through the bag I brought over to Tucker's.

"Pepperoni and pineapple is my favorite." He holds his hands out.

"My man." Tucker reaches over, giving him a high five.

I lift my nose up in disgust. "I only got the pineapple to make fun of it. Are the two of you both telling me you like pineapple on your pizza?"

"How dare you get pineapple just to make fun of it?" Tucker grabs his chest. "You barbarian."

"It's so good." Darren nods. "Sweet and salty."

Tucker and I look at each other, both of our mouths tilting in secretive smiles. He's too young to know just what's sweet and salty yet. We're in the middle of putting cheese on them when Ella lets out a strong wail.

"She's probably hungry." I immediately turn to wash my hands.

"I got this," Tucker tells me as he gets into her diaper bag, grabbing the bottle out.

There have been many things I've seen Tucker do. One thing I've never seen him do? Interact with a baby. I swear my stomach cramps together as I watch him pick her up gently, cooing to her as he snaps the seal on the bottle and mixes it together. He cradles her small body in his arms as he gently gets her to take the bottle. I've always known he's a gentle man, but I've never seen it quite like this before.

"Do we put them in the oven now?" Darren asks me, breaking the stare.

"Yeah." I clear my throat and my head. "They'll go in for about twenty minutes."

"SHE'S OUT," I whisper later on as Tucker and I sit on the couch.

We're watching a movie Darren picked out. Major is curled up at my feet, and I've been quietly bouncing Ella for the past twenty minutes.

"Looks like perfect timing." He moves the curtain behind the couch back. "They just rolled up."

Before we can get up, Nick comes through the door. "I could kill you, you bastard." He points to Tucker. "But you watched my kids, so I'll deal. You just wait though."

"What did he do?" Darren asks, looking between the two men.

"Nothing," Kels says as she comes in. "Nothing you need to worry about." She hits Nick on the shoulder. "You said you weren't going to say anything on the way over here."

"I changed my mind."

"Such a womanly thing for you to do." Tucker needles at him again.

"Next time we have to run the gauntlet," he refers to their obstacle course. "I'm gonna make sure you're behind me and eating my mud."

"Promises, promises big guy."

"Oh my God." Kels rolls her eyes. "Don't pay attention to him. We thank you so much for watching the kids." She comes over, taking Ella out of my arms.

"It was my pleasure. Helped me not think about all the stuff that's coming up."

I've told a few people about what's going on with my kidnapper, but I just don't like to talk about it.

"If you ever need to take your mind off of it again, you know where I am." She gives me a one-armed hug. "C'mon, D-man. It's almost time to get you into bed."

"Okay, but can I come over again sometime? I had fun with them, we made pizza and I got to play with Major."

I look at Tucker. This is his house, which means it's his decision. Neither one of us have ever talked about long-term. That's what got us so fucked up last time, and I refuse to be the one to make this decision.

"I'd love that." He grins at Darren. "Pineapple partners have to stick together."

"He finally found one, huh?" Nick shakes his head in disgust. "You two deserve each other."

As they drive off, Tucker and I watch them on his front porch, and when we turn in together, to go in. I wonder just how much longer this can last.

CHAPTER TWENTY-TWO

Tucker

"COME OUT WITH YOUR HANDS UP." I hold Major tightly in my grip. "If you don't, I'm sending in the dog and you will get bit."

Caleb stands beside me, his gun trained on the car we've chased through half of Laurel County. They wrecked out, and none of us can see in the car, all we can see is a little movement, and it doesn't sit well with any of us. There could be a gun in there, and we can't see it. "Do it one more time," he advises me.

"Driver! Come out with your hands up. If you don't I'm sending in the dog and you will get bit."

Major barks loudly, sounding ferocious even to me. That turns out to be the thing that makes the driver speak up.

"I'm coming out!" he yells.

We all watch on high alert as he shimmies his way out of the wreckage.

"Can you stand up?" Caleb questions.

"Yes, give me just a minute."

Once the driver stands up, Caleb calls out directions to him.

"Face away from us with your hands up. Take three steps back and go down to your knees."

I almost want to groan as I see the driver doing it. He has to be hurting. This crash is one of the worst I've ever seen.

"Cross your ankles."

"I'll get him." I walk forward with Major at my side. We cuff him, taking him into custody. "Is there anyone else in the car?" I ask as I help him up.

"No, it was just me."

"Well at least you didn't take someone else's life in your hands with this dumbass decision."

He doesn't say anything as I hand him off to Caleb. I listen as he's read his Miranda Rights, kicking at the glass scattered all over the road.

"This is gonna take a long fuckin' time to clean up." Ryan shakes his head as he comes over to stand next to me. "Such a damn waste."

I agree with him as we hear the wail of an ambulance. They park and I wave at Cutter. "What's up?"

"Working, like always." He rolls his eyes. "Where's my patient."

"In the back of Caleb's car. He doesn't appear to be too hurt, especially for the mess he's caused, but that's your job and not mine."

Major and I watch the cleanup of the scene, leaning against our SUV. The night's been pretty quiet, except for this. At some point, Nick arrived and walks over to where I'm standing.

"Still waiting on you to kill me," I tease him, nudging his shoulder.

"Dude, you're so lucky I like you."

I laugh loudly. "When did the first alarm go off?"

It's sick, but I really want to know. It's the best part of playing a prank.

"You fucker, it went off right as I slid inside."

"Damn." I raise my eyebrow. "You took some time with that foreplay."

He growls, his mouth set in a firm line. "Sometimes you have to, especially when you don't ever get a lot of time for it. To add onto all that shit, you fucker, it was my work phone. So I was freaking out when I couldn't find the damn thing. Almost lost my erection."

"Shit." I'm chuckling now, bent over at the waist.

"Kels was up, naked as hell, looking for it. I was trying to stay focused on finding the phone, but all I could watch were her swinging tits. I mean talk about being confused. I was torn by the two main parts of my life. You're an asshole, if I haven't already told you that. I'm telling you, I'm gonna get you back."

"I'm waiting on it." I cross my arms over my chest.

We're quiet for a few minutes and that's when I decide to delve into something a little more serious. "You heard any more about this possible escape at the prison?"

"No." He shakes his head. "Do you know how hard it was to keep her away from the LSERT meeting? Especially since you were working? Shopping with her is insane." He gives me a look. I'm not sorry I made him ask her for help in shopping for a gift for Kels. I just had to keep her away so she wouldn't know what could possibly be happening.

"Anyway, Caleb said they just don't have a good lead on

it. There's so many people it could be and there's not enough manpower to watch everyone closely. That's our biggest weakness right now, and I think everybody knows it."

"It is our biggest weakness, and you're right, I think everybody does know it. Sucks."

"You still worried about Karsyn?" He leans more against the SUV, his weight moving it back slightly so that I have to adjust my stance.

"I mean, wouldn't you be?"

"When does she go for the parole hearing?"

"Two days. Ryan's going to work for me. Ransom's gonna be on stand-by in case someone needs a K-9," I explain. "I'm not sure when we'll be back."

"If they need someone else, I'll put my name in the hat. This is important, you need to be there. I'll let Menace know at the end of my shift."

"Thanks, man." I reach out, shaking his hand. "I know I give you shit, but this is the best group of guys I've ever worked with."

"I don't know anything different." He shrugs. "Kinda makes me glad I don't."

"Trust me, Laurel Springs is special. Not a lot of departments run as well as this one does."

AFTER OUR SHIFT, Major and I pull up into my driveway, and like I've been doing lately, I smile as I see Karsyn's car sitting right next to where I pull my SUV in. She's made it a habit of staying here, and as we get closer to the parole hearing, I can't help but be glad she's made it a habit. I like having her in my arms every night, like knowing she's safe and not going anywhere.

"C'mon." I pull Major out of the back.

Quietly, we let ourselves in, turning the alarm off. He whines as he walks back to the bedroom. "Be quiet," I whisper to him, and it's just like he knows. "You sure you don't want to eat first?"

He makes a beeline for his food dish. Leaning down, I grab his food, pouring a generous amount into his bowl. I wait as he eats quicker than he probably should, and when he's done, we walk over to the back door, me letting him out. I leave the door slightly ajar, knowing he can shut it when he gets done and comes back in.

For a few minutes, I stand there watching him, making sure everything is okay, before I head back to take a shower. On nights like this, when I know Karsyn's in my bed, showers are short. I want to be with her more than I want to be clean. My arms ache to be wrapped around her, because I'm scared it's all going to come to an abrupt end.

Getting out, I wrap a towel around myself, doing my best not to make much noise. Entering the bedroom, I can see her, still sleeping, her eyes closed against the world. The muted light bathes her, giving her an angelic look.

Maybe I should tell her that she's my angel and she's saved me from myself? Then again maybe I should leave the sweet talk to Ransom.

Before I know it, Major's back in the bedroom, waiting on me to get ready for bed. Lately he's been sleeping in between us and I just don't have the heart to tell him no. It takes me a few moments to get ready, but once I am, I slip in between the cool sheets, while Major makes himself comfortable at our feet.

Karsyn comes to me in her sleep, wrapping herself around my body. I know she doesn't know how strongly she clings to me, but I love it. Love the fact she feels safe enough to know I'll protect her through her sleep, I'll watch her back no matter what dreams come to life. Her nails dig into my skin and I welcome the sting, because it lets me know she's fine, nothing bad has gotten to her.

"Tucker?"

"Yeah." I lean down, kissing her on the forehead. "It's just me, go back to sleep."

"Love you," she whispers, burrowing down deeper into my arms.

"Love you too," I whisper back.

And quietly I vow that I'll protect her. I'll slay the dragons and make sure she's in my arms for years to come. Because after these past few nights? I can't imagine living without her in my bed.

I've started counting on her being here when I wake up in the morning, when I go to sleep at night, and all the times in between. She's worked her way into my heart, into my life, and I don't want it to ever end. Even if that means making myself realize the thoughts I had before were wrong. It doesn't make me weak to love another person.

It makes me strong; for her I will come home at the end of every shift, and I'll make sure others are taken care of. With her by my side there's no way I can be selfish, I'll do everything it takes so that she's proud of me.

Karsyn makes me a better person, a better man, and a hell of a better cop, and it's time for to admit that to myself.

All the shit that was scary before? It's not scary now. I can imagine myself doing it all for her.

Wrapping her tightly in my arms, I breathe in her scent

deeply. So deeply it's ingrained in my soul, I never want to forget this night. How this feels, and how freely she gives herself to me.

What I don't know, is this night is what will keep me going when I'm not sure what the future holds.

CHAPTER TWENTY-THREE

Karsyn

"SHIT!" I hiss as I drop the tray with the freshly cleaned medical equipment on it. I fight against the tears that are pressing against the back of my eyelids.

"Are you okay?" Kels asks as she bends down, helping me pick them up.

My hands shake, and I hate it. Literally hate it more than anything at this point. "I'm fine." I angrily swipe at the tears that have squeezed past my eyes.

"No you're not. What's wrong?"

Since Kels became a mother, she's much more in tune with everything around her. I wouldn't say she feels more than she used to, because she's always been super emphatic. Now though? It's like times a thousand.

I have a seat on the floor because I can't seem to pick myself up from where I've bent down. "The hearing's tomorrow," I whisper.

"Already? For some reason I thought there were at least a couple more weeks," she sighs, having a seat next to me.

"I wish." I pull my bottom lip between my teeth, bringing my knees up to my chest, tucking my chin into them. I sigh heavily. "I remember when I first came here to work. You and Stella thought I had absolutely no common sense."

She snorts. "It wasn't that we didn't think you had common sense."

"No be honest, I was the newbie in your friendship and you both thought I was different, and I was," I concede.

"Okay, maybe we were slightly judgy."

"Slightly?"

"We were young," she defends again.

"Anyway, I know you two thought I had no common sense. That wasn't really the problem though. The problem was I'd never let myself have friends like you two before." I rub my cheeks on my scrub pants. "I was always so closed off to everyone and everything because of what happened to me."

She reaches over, clasping her hand over mine. "I heard," she whispers.

"I figured, everyone is clamoring to be the person to work for Tucker." I smile. "It's sweet, but I hate the reason everyone's being sweet."

Kels puts her arm around my shoulder, leaning our heads together. "Regardless of how Stella and I judged you, we both liked you a lot, and that's why we started inviting you to hang out with us."

"Thank God you did." I grin. "I wouldn't have had the guts to put myself out there with Tucker. The way I put my number on his ticket."

"He really pulled you over?" she asks.

"Yeah." I nod, giggling.

She leans in, wiping my tears. "You're gonna love telling that story to your kids one day, Karsyn. You're gonna be fine, ya know?"

"Am I?"

This time the tears come on strongly, and I'm sobbing as I tuck my forehead into Kels shoulder. She holds me as I let every bit of what's been bothering me over the past few weeks out. I haven't cried this way in years, and as I feel it coming to an end, I scrub my palms over my face, smearing every bit of makeup I applied this morning.

"You're going to be great. You'll have Shelby there with you, and Tucker. Are your parents coming?"

"No." I accept a tissue she hands me. "I haven't told them. They went through so much when I was a kid." I shake my head. "I just can't put them through this again."

"But you can put yourself through it?"

I see what she's saying, but it doesn't convince me I should tell them. All I've ever wanted to do is live a normal life, and more than anything I want them to be able to enjoy the time they have now. "I'm an adult now."

"But that doesn't mean we don't need our parents."

I smile over at her. "That's what I have you for, little mama."

She huffs out a breath as she glares at me. "I don't replace your mom and you know that."

"I know, but I appreciate everything you've done for me. You don't know how much you've helped me." I wrap my arms around her.

"Same," she answers. "When Stella decided to become a nurse, I was worried." She licks her lips, sitting up straighter, pulling her legs up under her crisscross style. "I was afraid I wouldn't have the type of friendship with her that we'd had before, and honestly we don't," she continues. "But I was afraid I'd be alone. You and I weren't incredibly close, and like you said, Stella and I had convinced ourselves you had no common sense." She blows out a barely contained laugh. "We were all in a place of growing." She pushes her hair back. "But I can say with complete sincerity, I'm glad you're here. My friendship with you isn't what it was with Stella, because she and I have known each other for so long, but it's still incredibly important to me. In some ways you're closer to me than she is, and vice versa. I wouldn't take anything for your friendship, Karsyn. I'm so glad we got to know each other."

I'm so surprised at what she's said to me, I don't know how to respond, other than to agree. "I am too, and you have no idea how much it means for you to tell me this. My life would be so empty without you and Stelle in it. I lucked out in the friend department."

"Same, which is why I'm telling you to go home. You don't know need to be here today."

"I can't leave you by yourself!"

"You can, because I'm telling you to. I happen to know Tucker's off. Go spend time with him before you have to confront your worst nightmare tomorrow. Lean on each other the way you should."

It takes me all of three minutes to realize she's right. I do need to lean on him, and if I don't, I'm going to regret it. "I love you." I hug her tightly.

"Love you too, Karsyn. Give him hell tomorrow. Don't let him push you around. I know you're stronger than that."

As I leave the clinic, I realize I am. I'm much stronger

than I ever thought I'd be. Maybe it just took someone telling me before I believed it.

I GO to the place I've been going more often than not lately. To Tucker's. When I pull into the driveway, I see his patrol SUV which means he's done for the day. Entering the house with the key he gave me, I look for him everywhere. It isn't until I hear Major bark that I think to go downstairs to the basement.

"Hey." I scratch Major's head as I carefully navigate the narrow stairs. "What's going on?" He whines, hitching his head toward the room I haven't been in yet.

When I get to the end of the stairs, I see a workout room. There are mirrors on the wall, a treadmill, a bike, and weight benches. Tucker is lifting weights, the veins in his arms straining, the tattoo on his side showing off with the sheen of sweat coating his body. A pair of low-slung sweatpants barely cling to his hipbones. There's no waistband for underwear, and given the way the material shows everything, I have to think he's not even wearing any. His eyes meet mine in the mirror, and I see the fire in his, even from where I stand. He doesn't stop lifting the weights, even as I step closer, he continues, counting with a rough grunt.

There's something between us, maybe it's the fact we aren't sure what's going to happen in the future, or just the animal magnetism I have to him, but I can feel as I get closer.

He's still counting, but then I hear a rough whisper of *fuck it* before he throws the weights to the ground.

Never in my life have I almost been tackled, and I am by him, his hands cup my face, pulling me into the hottest kiss

I've ever had. His lips devour me, his tongue fighting against mine as his fingers delve into my hair, tipping me farther back to his liking. My fingers try to get purchase on his skin, but it's slick and all they do is slide until I dig my fingernails into his flesh, holding on tightly. He finally pulls back, allowing me room to breathe. "What are you doing here?"

"Couldn't stay at work anymore, not with everything going through my head."

"Same, I couldn't stand around and wait." He crowds me, all up in my space pushing me toward the opposite wall. "Or sit as the case may be. I needed to do something, working out seemed to be the best option. But now that you're here," he palms my breast over my scrub top, "I'm thinking I have better ways for us to spend our time."

I'm completely on board, and let him know by hitching myself up, wrapping my legs around his waist. Without my feet in the way, he advances on the wall. I make a sound of surprise as my back comes into contact with it. He unhooks my legs from around his waist, and before I even know what's happened, I'm standing there in front of him in just a pair of matching bras and panties. The only thing he's wearing are the low-slung sweatpants I first saw him in.

"I haven't had lunch yet." He smirks.

"You haven't?" I'm completely confused.

"Nope, and I'm fuckin' hungry."

A squeal works its way from my throat as he hitches me up onto his shoulders, shoving his face in between my thighs.

"Oh my God," I moan, and as I look across the room, seeing our reflection in the mirrored wall, I realize this time? It's going to be one for the memory bank I'm never going to want to forget.

CHAPTER TWENTY-FOUR

Karsyn

UP above his shoulders I'm part scared, part turned on, which is causing the best kind of tickle in my stomach. Gripping his head in my fingers, I hang on tight as he moves the barrier of my panties aside and waits for what feels like a lifetime.

"C'mon, Tucker," I encourage him, sick of the anticipation.

"Patience." He blows against my clit, causing me to shiver.

I've never been the type of person to be patient when it comes to my pleasure. I want it when I want it, and he knows this. Just as I'm about to say something else to him, I feel his tongue flick against my flesh.

"Shit, Tucker." I tilt my head back against the wall, letting him do whatever he wants to me. He goes in hard, licking and sucking, doing all the things he knows will bring me to my knees (if I could go to my knees). When he hitches me up a bit higher onto one shoulder and drags a finger down my slit, slightly pressing it inside me, my eyes open widely. Is it in arousal? Surprise? I'm not sure which, but it's then I see myself in the mirror again.

I've never looked at myself like this before, never known how I appear to others in the throes of passion. My lips are full, bruised with the way he kissed me before, my hair tangled by his fingers, my thighs wide as he stands between them. I'm intrigued by the way I look, and want to see more.

"Keep going," I encourage him, thrusting against his tongue. It feels like an out-of-body experience as I watch the me in the mirror reach up and grab hold of one side of her bra. She pulls it down, exposing the flesh to the cold air in the room. The nipple tightens against the unexpected coolness, peaking. Before I even know what I'm doing, mirror me puts her fingers to the nipple, twisting it, before pressing her palm against it to soothe the burn. The orgasm takes me by surprise, and as I shake, I find myself back on my feet for a few moments, before I'm pushed to my knees.

My eager fingers tremble as I hook them into the waistband of his sweatpants, pulling them down. My hand wraps around his length, giving it a few test pumps before I hold on tight and push my lips down.

"Fuck, Karsyn," he breathes loudly.

Pressing his palms against the wall, he's almost in a push up position as he pushes into my throat. I'm eager as I take him down, hoping to give him as much pleasure as he gave me.

"Yes." He thrusts into me. "Use your tongue."

When I do, his body tightens and I wonder if he's trying not to come already. Pushing him out, I use my tongue to bathe the underside, before taking him down my throat again.

For long minûtes all that can be heard in the workout room is his grunts as he thrusts into me and my moans as I take him as much as I can. I can tell he's had enough when he reaches down, pulling me up by my chin.

"You ready, Syn?"

Because I no longer have a voice to give him what he's asking for, I nod.

He pulls me up by my ass, pushing me against the wall, he slips in just on the other side of my panties, shoving home as I moan, gripping my fingers against his back.

Opening my eyes, I'm treated to a glimpse of Tucker I never get. One of his body as he thrusts into me. He's got tattoos on his back - ones I've never really paid attention to, but as he thrusts into me, they move with the motion. The dimples at the top of his ass move along with the motion of his hips, and his ass, it gets tight, then gets release as he pushes home.

"Oh shit," I moan as his lips collide with my tight nipple, hanging out of the cup of my bra.

"Fuck yes," he mumbles against it as he thrusts harder, getting deeper than I imagined he could. "I love the way your body takes mine."

"Me too," I pant, tightening my legs around his waist.

This time when I look in the mirror, I take note of myself. The way my cheeks are pink, hovering just on this side of red. The way I hold my mouth open as he thrusts in and out of me. How when he hits a particular spot I love, I pull my lip in between my teeth and tilt my head back slightly. It's the most amazing thing I've ever seen. I've never known what I look like either. The way my eyes get super concentrated with the feeling of arousal Tucker inspires in me. I never realized how my fingers dig deeply into his skin, leaving imprints. Even from here I can see the scratches, and part of me loves that I'm leaving them there. Underneath his clothing, he wears a tattoo that's mine, it's one I've given him because he knows how to play my body like the fucking god he is.

"Syn," he breathes heavily, putting his face in my shoulder, "you feel so fucking good." He takes my throat in his teeth, nipping tightly before licking to soothe the bite he made.

"You feel fucking good too." I strain against him, loving the way he presses deeply into me, loving the way he's marking me too. If anyone will look tomorrow, I have no doubt they'll be able to see my hickey underneath the concealer I'll use to cover it up.

We push and pull against each other, both of us trying to get ours. He lets go of my leg, letting his body press me up against the wall. His thumb comes into contact with my clit, and as he picks up his pace, pressing against it with just enough pressure that I can feel myself starting the deep slide into oblivion.

"Tuck," I gasp.

"Yes, come for me," he growls in my ear. "Let me hear it, scratch my back, suck on my neck, press against me so hard I fall backward. Take what you want, take what you need, Syn. Do it."

I do exactly what he tells me to; I dig my nails into his back, scratching his flesh as I tilt my head to the side, pressing my mouth into his neck. My breathing is harsh and out of control as I feel myself losing the fight against not coming. He thrusts hard into me, holding the spot where he's abusing my clit with his thumb, and that's it.

Karsyn Fallaway, who's never screamed with an orgasm before, does exactly that as I bury my face in his neck, sucking, biting, thrusting against him. I can feel my leg locking, and as I try to straighten it out, I feel Tucker coming inside me, hot and hard. Somehow I get him off-balance and he does fall backward with me on top of him, which pushes him even further up into me, and makes me come again. He tries to touch me, but I'm so sensitive, all I can do is roll off of him and collapse into myself as my nerve-endings and everything else calm down. Never in my life have I felt anything like this.

We're both panting, each of us looking at the other, and the wonder of what we just went through is there. Neither one of us can seem to believe what the hell just happened. If It had been with anyone but him, I wouldn't even believe it at all, but I've always known Tucker owns a part of me that no one else has ever even so much as touched.

I don't know how he's managed to get so deeply into my psyche, but he has, and I'll thank God for it every day.

"Wow." I run a hand through my hair. "I didn't think that would happen when I came home early."

He laughs loudly, rubbing a hand against his stomach. "I didn't either. Believe it or not, as I was sitting there lifting weights, I was telling your kidnapper all the bad shit I was going to do to him, and then I saw you standing there in the mirror."

"That sounds like a good idea." I roll over onto my side. "What were the bad things you were going to tell him?"

"I'll kill him for hurting you if he gives me the chance."

I scoot over, putting my head on his shoulder, hugging

him to me tightly. "I love you, and I appreciate you being willing to kill him for me, but I don't want you to get in trouble."

"I'd do anything for you. I was stupid a year ago," he sighs. "So fucking dumb, like I couldn't get out of my own way dumb. I'm sorry we broke up."

"I'm not." I look up at him. "Breaking up was what we needed to do to be where we are right now, and if that's the case, I'll take it any day over what the alternative is. I'd much rather be with you, than without you."

He makes a noise of agreement. "I don't know about you, but I worked up an appetite."

My laugh is loud and without the worry I've heard in it the last few days. "I could eat."

"Then c'mon." He grabs my hand, helping us both stand up. "Let's go eat."

CHAPTER TWENTY-FIVE

Tucker

I DON'T KNOW whose more nervous, me or Karsyn. I'm holding her hand in a death grasp as we drive toward the federal facility in Birmingham. Neither one of us slept last night. I felt like we were awake every hour asking if the other was okay.

"Talk to me," she whispers. "I need you to talk to me."

It feels like I don't have anything to talk about, but I search for anything to put her at ease.

"The first time I saw you, I knew you were going to be mine." I grin over at her.

She rolls her eyes blowing out a breath. "Sure you did."

"No, I did. I told Ransom that night after I gave you the ticket, I was going to date you. When I told him your name, he gave me the rundown on you working at the clinic."

"Yet, you still didn't call me, even though I left my number on the ticket," she teases.

"Let's be honest, I get flirted with a lot since I'm a man in uniform. I didn't think I was anything special, and it was presumptuous of me to call," I admit.

"What did you tell him?" She seems genuinely interested.

"That you were beautiful, and the way you got mad when I gave you the ticket got me slightly hard. If you can't tell, I love it when you stand up for yourself."

"Oh I can tell."

"For the next few days I wondered when I would see you again, even patrolled that stretch of highway looking for you, hoping you'd go flying by with your lead foot. You never did though."

"Learned my lesson and couldn't afford another ticket," she laughs.

"When I walked into the grocery store and saw you there, I knew my luck was changing."

"Meanwhile I was like, he can't fuckin' call me, but he found me at the grocery store."

I chuckle, bringing her hand up to my lips. "Matter of opinion, my love."

"Matter of opinion," she agrees, turning toward me in her seat.

"There's also the night I knew I loved you."

This one is going to take us back, is going to have me admitting I was an asshole last time we were together.

"When was that?" She tilts her head to the side, those eyes of her so expressive with the interest of knowing my intimate feelings. I get it, I hardly ever tell her what's going on in my head.

"The first night we were together."

She scrunches up her nose. "Like our first date?"

"No, the first night we had sex." I stop talking for a

minute. "There was just something about the way you made me feel." I'm searching for the words. "I knew I was in deep, I knew you were it for me, but I couldn't say it. Still almost can't."

"I thought so." She tightens her fingers around mine. "I didn't think I was the only one who felt it that night, which is why I was so pissed when you broke up with me."

We're getting into territory I've never been in with anyone else. "I didn't have the best childhood growing up, like Nick and I have a lot in common, in more ways than being cops. I understood where he was coming from, and that's kind of as far as I wanna go into it. Before you, love meant hurt and angry words back and forth. I knew immediately it wouldn't be like that with you. There were too many things going on in my head though, I couldn't give you every part of me, while I was trying to save myself the hurt I knew would eventually come."

"You hurt me before I could hurt you," she finishes up.

"Exactly." I nod, not proud of how I handled the first part of our relationship. "If I could go back and prevent that year from happening I would."

"I wouldn't," she cuts in. "It made me grow up, made me realize that you can love someone and still lose them. It made me stronger in ways I never imagined I could be. Even though it was painful, and at the time I didn't think I'd ever get over it, I'm thankful for it, Tucker. Just like I'm thankful for you. We may not be perfect, but we love each other in ways no one else has ever loved us, and that's all that matters."

"Damn right." I lift her hand to my lips again.

"This is the exit." She points, her hand shaking.

We can see the facility from the road, and I can feel the

fear coming off her in waves. This is what I wanted to prevent for her. If I'm being honest, though maybe she needs to feel this fear to be strong enough to face what she's facing in the next little while.

"That's where he is," she whispers. "Where he's been held, I never realized how close it actually was to me."

"You know I'd never let him get any closer to you than that, right?"

"I know what we believe might happen." She swallows so roughly I can see it. "But I'm also a realist. We can't prevent things that are bound to happen, and he's kidnapped before."

"He's also never met me." I give her the look I give when someone I pulled over is giving me a hard time.

But as we go through the gate, I almost wonder if she's right.

Karsyn

EVEN THOUGH THE temperature is typical Alabama in late spring, I'm freezing. My hands are shaking and my teeth are almost chattering. It's a reaction to shock and anxiety, I know that more than anything, but it still doesn't make it much easier.

"You're going to be fine." Tucker grabs my hand in his as we walk to the entrance.

I've dressed nicely today because I want to be taken seriously, but now I'm questioning whether it was a good idea or not. I'm worried that I'm showing too much knee and leg, second guessing all my damn decisions. This is what the man behind those bars makes me do. For years I replayed what happened to me. Could I have done something to prevent it? Had I seen it coming and not been able to stop it? Only years of therapy stopped the blame game I was doing with myself.

"Are you okay?" Tucker asks as we walk into the lobby.

"As okay as I can be." I grip my fingers in front of me tightly, digging my fingernails into my flesh. It's keeping me grounded, taking me outside of where I am now, letting me focus on things other than this moment.

I don't even remember telling the people at the desk why we're here, or what we're doing. I don't realize we're going through metal detectors, not very cognizant of what is actually happening. It's not until we get to the room and take a seat that I look around, realizing exactly where I am.

It's a small room, and the claustrophobia I developed after the abduction threatens to rear its ugly head.

"You're amazing," Tucker is whispering in my ear. "I don't know I could be as strong as you are. You're a rock star, Karsyn."

Part of me wants to yell at him, hit his chest and tell him to stop placating me, not to talk about me like I'm not here. I don't feel any of these things.

Out of nowhere, Shelby appears at my side. "I made it." She gives me a smile. "And I brought the statement we prepared."

She really doesn't have to be here, I was told that when I called to let them know I would be speaking at the hearing. In fact, they say it would probably be best that she didn't come, but after meeting with her, I feel stronger in my convictions. She helped me prepare a statement I'm proud of, and I wanted her here to witness it. I just need a strong woman to look out into the crowd and lock eyes with. She's done so many things that others told her she probably wouldn't be able to do because she's a woman in a man's world. I need the confidence her accomplishments have given her, to help me with mine.

"Thank you." I reach over, grabbing the very wrinkled piece of paper.

I labored over what I wanted to say. My thoughts were so jumbled and they honestly didn't have any kind of cohesiveness to them. Luckily for me, she knew what I wanted to say, what I wanted to convey to people who have no idea the hell I went through.

"It's seen better days," Tucker comments as he looks at the paper in my hand.

I close my eyes, visualizing what's on the white sheet. There are dried tears, scribbled out words, a complete piece of my heart in written form. A piece of myself I didn't know I needed to give voice to.

Thanks to Shelby, I've given voice to it, and I'm anxious to stand in front of these people, making the most important decision of my life, and tell them exactly what it will mean to not only me, but any other victims, if he's let free.

For once I want to be the strong voice standing up for the future. Not the weak one, living in my past. It's hard, and it's not exactly who I am now, but it's who I promise I will be from now on. If I can help even one person, it will be worth it, because not long ago; I was one person. The person he kidnapped and took without her consent. And I'll be damned if I let that happen to someone else on my watch.

These words? They're powerful and they're mine.

CHAPTER TWENTY-SIX

Karsyn

IT'S BEEN years since I've seen Clarence Night, fourteen to be exact. He looks different than I imagined. The last fourteen years he's remained the same way he was the day he kidnapped me. His hair a light brown, skin tanned by the sun, clean-shaven, and muscles honed by doing whatever he did before he took me.

I'm unprepared for the man who walks out with his hands shackled to his feet. While these last fourteen years have been good for me, it's obvious they've been awful for him. Gone is the light brown hair, replaced with gray and greasy splotches of white, the skin that was once vibrant now has a pallor almost looking jaundiced, the muscles he used to hold me still and silent aren't there anymore either. He's a shell of the man he once was, and while I thought I'd be happy about that, I'm not. I feel sorry for him in a way. Yes, what he did scarred me, but at least I got to live.

Looking at him?

He never did.

That doesn't sway me though, I still have a story to tell, and I'm damn well going to tell it.

I take stock of what's in front of me and acknowledge the differences from what I imagined this moment would be. Instead of the orange prisoner jumpsuit, he's dressed nicely in a button-down shirt and a pair of slacks, probably to try and prove he's changed his ways. For the first time, I look around the room. There's a table at the front, two men and one woman sit facing us. Another table directly in front of us. He looks at me as he passes that table, before he turns his back.

Tucker grips my hand hard, and I grip his back with the same amount of force. This is harder than I ever imagined it would be. Clarence takes a seat at the very end, his shackles making loud clinking noises in the silence. I desperately want someone to speak. The silence is thundering in my head, so loud I almost want to put my hands over my ears to block it out.

After what feels like an eternity, one of the men begins to speak.

"This is a parole hearing for Clarence Night. We're going to start the hearing for the record by going around the room, stating who all is here."

I listen as they introduce his attorney, the parole board members, and then my advocate stands up when asked.

"Karsyn Fallaway, who is the victim of the crime."

Again I shake, closing my eyes. Tucker has his arm around me, his other hand in mine, and is literally giving me his warmth, his courage, and the fortitude I need to do this, when all I really want to do is run.

I do my best to block out everything as I hear the parole

board start to speak. They're asking Clarence if he has a statement, and of course he does.

It's shocking to hear his voice again after so many years.

"I'd like to thank the parole board for their time, and my attorney for helping me prepare this statement. Sometimes I can't put into adequate words what I want to say."

I just bet you can't.

"In the past fourteen years I've become a changed man."

Would it be wrong to laugh?

"The man who went to prison was one who didn't know right from wrong. Coming from the childhood I did, where I was beaten for doing any little thing my dad perceived to be a slight on him, or verbally smacked down by my mother every single day, I had a warped sense of what was expected of me. A middle school drop-out, I didn't even have the basic skills many teenagers have. Keep in mind, I was twenty-seven when the crime occurred."

I take a deep breath, trying not to let what he's saying get to me.

"All I knew that hot, summer day was that I needed a friend. Yes, Karsyn," I legitimately shudder when he says my name, "was much younger than me, and I should have known better, but I didn't. Loneliness had gotten the best of me; I'd spent my entire life lonely. I wanted a partner, someone to spend my time with, whether it be for three hours, or the rest of my life."

I always knew he wanted me forever.

"I was a selfish man, and I can't say enough how sorry I am about that now. I'm saved." He makes a sound like he's laughing. "And I know my God has forgiven me."

I want to throw up.

"In closing, I hope that you would too."

Anger courses through my body at such a fast pace, I'm not sure I can even stand it. I don't think I've ever hated anyone as much as I do the man in front of me. I thank the God he just praised so much that I can't see his face.

"Would you like to say anything?" one of the men up front asks his attorney.

"No, I believe Mr. Night said everything he needed to say."

The lone woman up there searches me out in the crowd. "I believe Ms. Fallaway has a prepared statement?"

"She does." Shelby's voice is firm, exactly what I need to hear at this moment.

She grips my other hand, helping me stand. She stands right along with me, and it was the thing I didn't know I needed.

My hands are shaking, and I'm doing my best to keep my voice level. I don't want him to know how much all of this still affects me.

"I was thirteen years old when Mr. Night kidnapped me," I start, trying to keep the tears back. "I was walking to a friend's house to see her new puppy." I stop for a moment. "Think about that. I was a thirteen-year-old, walking to a friend's house to see her new puppy. I know I didn't start that walk out thinking I'd be kidnapped by a man who would take me to a hotel, force me to change in front of him," my voice cracks right then and I fucking hate it, "dye my hair a different color, and then subject me to forty-eight hours of complete terror while a manhunt ensued."

Because of Shelby we had a little bit of an idea as to what Clarence was going to plead for his parole, and I'm able to answer some of the points he made.

Gripping the paper tighter, I clear my throat, sniffing

loudly. "I find it hard to believe that a twenty-seven-year-old with a middle school education, who didn't know right from wrong, knew to change my clothes, knew to change my hair, and also knew to put the fear of God in me. That God you vow to serve now, Mr. Night. I wonder does that God know you have 'poison' tattooed on your penis? Does he know you forced me to watch you pleasure yourself while I sat inches away from you? Have you confessed to that God that you had me touch myself while you watched? For so long you've held the fact that you never did anything sexual to me up like it's some sort of trophy, when really you forced me to do it to myself. Do you understand how messed up I was about that? How it took me until my early twenties to realize it's okay to want love and sex? Do you get that it took years of counseling for me to get that memory of your poison out of my mind?"

I stop for a second, accepting a tissue and taking in a shuddering breath.

"So excuse me if I don't believe for one second you're sorry. You aren't sorry. You haven't found God. What you've done is you've moved south. Away from Tennessee and to the middle of southern Alabama and someone has convinced you finding Jesus is going to get you parole. God knows." I tilt my head back. "God knows you are an evil man who doesn't deserve it. He knows what you did to me during those forty-eight hours. The things neither one of us want to talk about, and he knows you're dirty, he knows you're doing nothing but trying to save yourself, and he knows exactly what's in your heart. And that's pure evil."

It takes me a minute to calm my racing heart, to center myself, and to be able to look at the parole board.

"He will do this again," I tell them in a calm voice.

"Because that's the type of man he is. He told me during my time with him that he'd tried it three times before and he'd never been lucky enough to get a girl. Just so happened, he was able to take me. He will without a doubt do this again. Please don't give him a chance to. He's sick, he's perverted, and he's a drain on society. We have enough of that out in the world without adding someone else."

I have a seat and wait, my hand clasped in Tucker's as I wait for what the board is going to say. It feels like an eternity until I hear the words I've been waiting for all day.

"Clarence Night, your parole is denied."

I don't make a sound. I just get up from my seat and walk to the door, but when I turn back, he's looking at me and I get a feeling; this isn't the last time I'll see him.

CHAPTER TWENTY-SEVEN

Tucker

I WATCH Karsyn stand up to deliver her victim impact statement, proud as hell of her. I know how hard this was, could tell in the way she became quiet on me in the past few days. Withdrawing into herself is a coping mechanism and I allowed it, but after this I want her to be one thousand percent honest with me about what's going through her head.

As her voice shakes, I reach over from where I sit, beside her, rubbing my hand up and down her back. I don't want to take anything away from what she's doing, but I want her to know I'm here.

Anger is making it almost impossible for me to sit without making a sound, though, as she mentions things she's never told me. Not that I ever expected her to tell me every bit of what happened to her while she was with him, but I'm angry. Angry enough I'd like five fucking minutes alone with this piece of shit.

She's crying now, and it's literally tearing me apart. I hate to hear that vulnerable lilt to her voice. It upsets me to know she's upset. I have to keep reminding myself, this isn't about me. This is about her and what she's been through. This is Karsyn's truth, and it doesn't matter what I feel like I can take. She's lived with it for longer than she's known me, and the least I can do is be her strength when she needs it most.

My heart is pounding as I sit there, waiting to hear what the parole board will say. She's sat back down, and I've put my arm around her shoulders, pulling her body into mine, taking her hand, silently telling her everything will be okay.

The words *parole denied* are my fucking favorite.

Together we stand, leaving the room, and that man behind.

When those doors close, I pull her up into my arms, holding her tightly. I can feel her tears against my flesh, and quite possibly there are tears slipping down my cheeks too.

"I love you," I whisper to her, putting my hands on her cheeks. "You're safe and I love you. Nothing is ever going to happen to you again." I tilt her face so that I can kiss her.

It's a small peck, nothing like what we normally have, but it's enough to let her know how I'm feeling.

"I love you too," she cries, holding tightly to me.

We stand there for seems like forever as the emotions flow through both of us. Eventually, we start to get it together, and Shelby appears out of nowhere, offering me a tissue for Karsyn. I do something I've never done for her or any other woman. I clean her up.

Carefully, I sweep up the tears under her eyes, taking care to get the dark mascara that's smudged. Then I get her cheeks and her jawline, fixing up her makeup as best I can. I don't care how she looks, she's beautiful any way I can get her, but I know she cares. More than anything I want her to be comfortable, want her to not have to worry.

When she's done, she takes a heaving breath, before looking at me. "Can we go home?"

Those are the best words I've ever heard. I don't even think I knew I needed to hear them. "Yeah." I push her hair back from her face, hating to stop touching her. I'm afraid if I stop this will all disappear. "Yeah, we can go home."

We leave, hand in hand, the way we came in, and as the prison gets smaller in my rearview mirror, I hope like hell I never have to see it again.

"WHERE ARE YOU GOING?" she asks as we pull into Laurel Springs. Typically to get to my house I'd turn left, to get to hers I'd turn right. I turned right, and she probably thinks I'm dropping her off.

I do the best I can to suppress my grin. "I have an errand to run."

"Right now?" She looks around.

It's well past time for me to be running errands. The sun having set an hour ago, but it's all just part of the plan.

"Yeah, I mean you know I don't have a normal schedule. Sometimes I have to do things when it's convenient. Since I didn't have to work today, I have extra time that I hadn't counted on."

She's confused as hell, I can see it in the way she scrunches up her nose, causing a wrinkle in her forehead. I come to a stop at a stop sign.

"Don't do that." I reach over, smoothing out the wrinkle. "It'll give you wrinkles."

There she is. The spitfire I much prefer over the quiet, sullen woman riding back with me tonight.

"Seriously, Tuck? That's a real shitty thing to say."

She's still laying into me as we pull onto Main Street, in front of where The Café sits.

"What's going on here?" I interrupt her tirade.

Karsyn stops, taking in the amount of cars that are parked on the street. Typically our town would be rolling the carpet up at this time of night, instead of filling The Café to the brim.

"Tuuucckkkerrr? What is this?" She turns to me.

"I don't know why you're lookin' at me. We've been together since yesterday." I notice an empty spot has been left at the entrance. Parking there, I go over to open her door.

"Are you sure you don't know what this is?" she asks, glancing inside, but the shades are drawn, so neither of us can see what we're walking into.

"All I know is a lot of this town loves you, Syn, and you're special to many people. Whatever this is, just let them do it."

"Ha! I knew you knew something was going on."

Grabbing her hand, I pull her behind me as we walk up to The Café door. "I'm starving," I tell her.

"I just bet you are," she laughs.

As soon as we step over then threshold, lights pop on and we hear a loud *Congratulations!*

Instead of watching the amount of people who have showed up, I watch Karsyn. Tears, this time ones of joy and happiness, pool in her eyes. She's slapped her free hand over her mouth, and I can tell by the shaking of her shoulders she's giggling.

"What is this?" she screams, looking at Kels and Stella.

Major barks from where he's sitting with Ransom and Rambo. He makes a mad dash across the floor, almost tackling her with the excitement of seeing her, after us being gone all day.

Kels and Stella run across the room with him, each taking her up in their arms.

If I'm not mistaken, I see both of them wiping at tears under their eyes.

"We're so happy for you," Kels tells her. "And all of us," she extends her arm around the room, "wanted to show you how happy we are that you chose us to be your home after everything that's happened. This night is for you, my friend, please enjoy it."

She's crying again, but her friends take her up in their arms. I stand over to the side, shooting the shit with Nick while I watch her make the rounds. There are people I know, and ones I don't. From what I was told, even patients who love her were invited.

There are two people she stops and talks to for a long time, an older couple, and I wonder if this is her parents. She and I, we never got to the point where we were going to meet each other's families. At least not in our previous relationship.

"You gonna meet the parents tonight?" Nick asks, nudging me with his elbow.

"I didn't even know they were invited." I scrub at my chin with my hand. A nervous gesture I've picked up lately.

"I knew they were going to be invited." He winks.

Throwing my head back, I cross my arms over my chest. "This? This is my fucking payback? You're an asshole."

"So are you," he fires back at me. "I mean don't act like you're sitting there on a moral high horse. You interrupted what was supposed to be uninterrupted sex with me and my wife. This isn't the last of your payback, my man. Not by a long shot."

I groan deep in my throat, immediately feeling my palms get wet as I watch them walk over toward where we stand.

I have *never* met the parents before.

Not even once. In any relationship I've been in.

But as she gets closer and I look into her green eyes, I see how badly she wants me to meet them, how badly she wants this to work. I'd be lying if I said different. More than anything I want us to be happy with one another, to have the relationship we've both deserved.

So when they get close enough that she can reach out and take my hand, I give it to her. There's no hesitation on my part. I'm diving head first, completely fearless in what's about to happen, because I've come to realize the only that can hold me back is fear.

I've let fear rule my life too long.

Happiness needs to be at the forefront now, and I know there's one person who makes me happy above the rest of them.

Karsyn Fallaway, with the smile on her face and love in her eyes.

CHAPTER TWENTY-EIGHT

Karsyn

TODAY MUST BE the day for facing fears and coming out on the other side, because I'm doing something I never thought I'd do: I'm walking my parents over to where Tucker stands and I'm going to introduce them.

This reminds me of when we were first together. There was no way we would be in this situation. He wouldn't have allowed it, and I'm not sure I would have subjected him to it, but now? After everything that's happened today, I want him to meet them. I want them to know I'm in good hands, and what a great guy he is.

"Tucker." I reach out, taking his hand in mine when I get close enough. "I'd like for you to meet my parents, Melinda and Pruitt Fallaway."

My heart literally could burst out of my chest when I hear them exchange pleasantries.

"You're a K-9 Officer?" my dad asks, his voice all tough and full of gravel in his throat.

"Yes, sir." Tucker rocks back slightly on his feet. A habit I've noticed he does when he's explaining his job. "I'm the K-9 trainer and also an officer with the Laurel Springs Police Department, and I'm also a member of the Laurel Springs Emergency Response Team."

"We weren't sure whether Karsyn would be a good fit for that." Mom shows her worries, pushing her hair back from her face.

"Karsyn has done amazingly with it. We're actually having a bake sale and a car wash next week to raise money for a new K-9. She's heading that up, even with everything that's been going on." He looks over at me. There's no mistaking the pride in his eyes.

"You take on too much," Dad reprimands like he always does.

Somehow he's afraid if I overextend myself I'm going to have a relapse of some sort.

"I do not, but you're welcome to come help us wash cars." I give him a grin. "Tucker's helping."

"I'm sure he is." Dad pats his stomach. "But let's be honest. Most people will be there to see men like him, and not men like me."

Those words turn out to be the ones that break the awkwardness between the four of us. That joke makes us all laugh, and later on as we have seats across from each other at a booth, I'm in awe this is my life.

"He seems really nice," Mom says after Tucker and Dad get up to go get us food to eat.

"He is." I smile as I watch him talking with my dad. I should have known he would be fine with him, with the profession he has he talks to people every day, but there's something about watching the man I love talk to my dad.

"He's the best. I can't believe everyone planned this without me knowing."

"I have to say," she chuckles. "It was scary when a Laurel Springs Police Department patrol car pulled up in our driveway, but Nick was super sweet to invite us."

When she says Nick, I know exactly why they were invited. It was payback. I cough, trying to hide the laugh. "Nick is super sweet. He's married to my co-worker Kels."

"They have the baby, right?" She takes a sip of her drink.

"They have a baby and so do Stella and Ransom. Stella worked with me too, until she went full-time at the hospital," I explain, relaxing against the booth. "Ransom's family owns The Café."

"Babies seem to be in the water." She winks at me.

"They are," I answer. "For the ladies with rings on their fingers and husbands."

"Do you have something to tell me?"

"No." I shake my head, looking back over at Tucker and Dad. "When I do have something to tell you, I'll let you know. Right now we're just trying to make it through life, ya know?"

She reaches over, grabbing my hand in hers. "I get that, Karsyn, but I do wish you had told me and your dad about what happened today. We would have loved to be there for you."

It's hard to explain to her what I'm feeling, but I do my best. "I didn't want you to go back to those forty-eight hours," I explain.

"But you would allow yourself to?"

"You and Dad had to uproot your entire life. You may not think I realize it, but I know how badly we struggled because the house wouldn't sell, and we had to get one here.

I heard the two of you talking about how bad it was sometimes, when you thought I was asleep. There was no reason for me to bring you back to that."

She clears her throat. "Things were hard, Karsyn. Because that's life. Something else could have possibly made us have to move. It might not have had anything to do with you. We never once blamed you."

"I know." I squeeze her hand. "And I thank you so much for that, I blamed myself enough. I know it wasn't cheap to put me in counseling and to make sure we had an alarm system. I'm aware of all the sacrifices you made."

"I'd make them again," she assures me. "Any day of the week I'd make them again just to make sure you felt safe. For a long time we blamed ourselves. We shouldn't have left you home."

"I was thirteen," I argue.

"But still a child. It was our job as parents to protect you and we felt like we failed so acutely. When the two of us finally got into counseling, after you talked about how much it helped you, we were able to learn all the parts of grieving. The loss of your innocence and ours too, really. Before that afternoon we assumed we lived in a safe place, we thought we could leave you there unattended."

"I remember how long it took for me to feel safe to stay by myself again."

"Years," she sighs. "And we only went one street over," she admits. "We were supposed to go to dinner and a movie. That's what we'd planned and promised to do, but neither of us could stand to be that far away from you. Not after what happened. We went one street over and parked there until it was supposedly time for us to come home."

I laugh loudly as I think about that night. "I sat in front

of the door with a baseball bat in my hand. For those three hours, I silently dared anyone who was on the outside to come and get me. I was scared to death, like, shaking so badly."

"I never would have known; when we got home you acted like it hadn't been any big deal."

Thinking back, I remember how much I'd wanted to be normal, how I'd wanted them not to worry about me anymore. How I'd wanted to not worry about myself. "It was hard." I can admit that now. "But I wanted to be normal. I was done letting fear control my life."

"Looks like you've done the same thing with Tucker." She nods over to him.

"I have." I grin. "Things are good with him, and I'm so glad you got to meet him."

"Me too."

Dad and Tucker come back over, carrying our plates. A little spot in my stomach warms as I look at what he's gotten me. All my favorite foods, except for the small piece of cake he has on his plate.

"What the crap, Tuck? No cake for me?"

He taps my nose. "I know you better than you think I do. Had I brought you the cake now, you would have eaten it first. Neither one of us have eaten today, so you don't need sugar, you need real food. Eat the real food and we'll split the sugar."

"Oh my God, you have been paying attention."

"More often than you think I do, but you just keep thinking I'm not, babe. Maybe I'll be able to surprise you a bit more."

"Maybe you will," I agree.

He leans over, whispering in my ear. "But maybe you

should eat most of the cake. I gotta watch my figure for that car wash next week."

I pinch his waist. "You are so full of it!"

His arm goes around my neck, pulling me into him, and as I sit in the booth, hip to hip with him, I can't think of any other place I'd rather be.

CHAPTER TWENTY-NINE

Tucker

"YOU'RE LYING," I laugh so loudly I have to hold my side.

"Hand to God." Ransom holds up the hand he's talking about. "First fuckin' time it's ever happened."

"You're lucky, then." I wipe at my eyes.

We're in one of the meeting rooms the Laurel Springs PD uses, and we're waiting for everyone else to get here. He's telling me about the night he had with Stella.

"Lucky my ass!"

I laugh again. "More like nose up your ass."

"Did you tell him about it?" Nick grins as he sits next to us, drinking an energy drink.

"Yes!" I blow out a breath trying to keep my shit together.

"At least you didn't get a phone call at 5 a.m. this morning.

"You called him at 5 a.m.?" I give Ransom a look.

"He was up with the baby," he defends. "And so was I, plus I had to share with someone."

"Not sure I'd share with my wife's brother, but you do you, fam."

"What the fuck are you ladies making so much noise about?" Caleb comes in, having a seat in front of us, but turning around so that he can be in on the conversation.

Ransom huffs, but gets ready to tell the story again. "So last night Stella was off, I'd had the day off too. I cleaned, made her dinner, made sure Keegan was good. He went down super easy and early. She drank a glass of wine, I had some whiskey and I was like *fuck yeah, I'm gonna get some tonight.*"

Caleb laughs. "Famous fuckin' last words my man."

"Right?" Nick laughs along with him. "One day he'll learn."

I give Nick a look, reminding him of what I did on the last night him and Kels spent together.

"So anyway, she's a little tipsy, I'm a little tipsy, we're doing a few things we haven't done since the baby." He scratches his chin, before tilting his head back. "In the middle of it, I thought I heard something, you know, like a door opening. I forget about it though, I set the alarm. It hasn't made any noise, we're good. So I keep on, when all of a sudden, I feel something wet at my ass. At first I'm like, it's just sweat, no big deal, but then I realize it's cold, and it's moving. I try to ignore it, but it keeps on, and I'm like what the fuck is happening? I stop, turn around, and fucking Rambo is on the bed, sniffing around like he's looking for a goddamn bone."

"Well," Nick holds onto my shoulder as he bends over at the waist, laughing, "he kinda was."

"Real fuckin' funny." Ransom flips him a middle finger.

"I mean I thought so." He's still laughing and I can't help but laugh too.

"You two leaning into each other like you're a couple of old women." Ransom folds his arms over his chest.

"Don't get butt hurt." Caleb's grinning too.

"He can't when his dog is sniffing it." I crack up hard this time, not sure why I'm laughing so much.

"I hate you all." He gets up, going to sit a few seats over.

"Ransom," Nick purses his lips, throwing him a kiss and a wink, "you know we love you."

He turns his head. "Not talking to any of you fuckers."

Mason comes in, giving us a glance as he walks up to the front of the room. "I don't even want to know what you guys are talking about, but I'm gonna need you to tighten it up."

"Yeah," Caleb says to his Dad. "That's what Ransom needed too."

The group erupts again. There have been so many days and nights of us all being on edge, trying to figure out what was going to happen with Karsyn. Now that she's okay - I especially - feel like I can breathe again.

"WE'VE GOTTEN some more information from our prison informant," Mason continues as he stands in front of us. So far the meeting has been just like any of our normal ones, but this news makes me sit up a little taller. "The escape looks to be a go. We're still unsure of when and how, but I need you all to be ready to report."

I make a note to talk to Karsyn about this. She's been feeling a little more freedom in the past few days since the parole hearing and with whatever this may be, I'd rather for her to be safer than sorry.

"Any questions?" he asks as he goes to end the meeting.

"Yeah." I raise my hand. "Are you coming to help us wash cars this afternoon."

"Shit," he sighs. "Is that this afternoon?"

Everybody in the room answers him with a yes.

"I feel like y'all would get more money without me there."

"Oh c'mon, old man," Caleb ribs him. "You know there's plenty of ladies out there that like a silver fox."

"There's also your mom who would kick my ass if she thought I was helping just for my ego."

"Dad's coming," Nick mentions. "So you won't be the only one out there with some silver showing."

"You young shits are going to be the death of me." He runs a hand through his still-thick hair. "Yeah, put me on the list."

"I'll have Karsyn send you a time."

"Okay, y'all get to work."

Normally we'd all be heading for our patrol cars, but today our work is a little bit different.

Karsyn

"BRING it just a smidgen to the left," I tell Kels as she helps us set up for the car wash. We have a booth where people can have their pictures taken with Rambo and Major. "There ya go!"

With that step, we're done. All we need is for the guys to show up and help get the public here.

"Do you even feel the least bit guilty for subjecting your boyfriend's body?" Stella asks, hitching Keegan up on her hip.

"Nope, not even a little. While everyone else is watching him work in no shirt, I will also be watching him work with no shirt," I smirk. "Win-win for me."

"True, do you like my tank top and his shirt?" She moves Keegan so I can see what's printed on it.

Ransom is my baby daddy. Rambo is my big brother.

I roll my eyes, but can't help the giggle that comes out. "Staking claim, I see?"

"I mean after those Facebook posts when we were dating? I will always stake claim when it comes to my man."

Those messages were so long ago in the grand scheme of things, but I can tell Stella is sincere in her statement. "Just don't threaten anyone who looks at your husband with lust."

"I'll do my best."

"Your parents are going to be here to watch the kids, right?" I confirm with her, looking again at my clipboard.

"Yep," she confirms. "They texted before I left, they're going to get some water and snacks, in case we need them. They should be here shortly."

"Awesome! My parents are on their way. They went to the bank to get change for us."

"They're working the entrance and exit?" she asks.

"Yeah, Mom will be in charge of taking the money, and Dad's gonna be directing traffic."

"Here's the real question." She winks. "Who will be holding the sign to let people know we're actually doing this today?"

"Caleb and his kids." I wink back at her.

"Oh my God! You really went for the heart with that

one, considering Levi is the spitting image of Caleb and Mason."

"I know, he's young, but he's super cute. Molly looks like Ruby, and let's face it - Caleb is a DILF. With them all standing out there, we should get really good traffic."

"We should get really good traffic regardless, everybody in this community loves to support the guys. You did a great job of planning this."

"You think so?"

Stella and Kelsea's opinions always mean the most to me because I've looked up to them since I started working with Dr. Patterson. I try not to let it show a lot, but sometimes I'm more transparent than I want to be.

"Yeah." She grins. "You've come into your own these past few months, Karsyn. I know Kels and I used to joke about you."

"No." I shake my head. "You two were kind of right, but it wasn't because I didn't have common sense, it was because I was scared to trust myself."

"Well," she puts Keegan down, hugging me tightly, "you should always trust yourself. You're a very smart and beautiful woman who doesn't get the credit you deserve."

Keegan looks up at me, holding his arms up. I grin down at him. "You want me?"

It's taken him a bit longer to talk. They found out recently he needed tubes and more often than not couldn't hear. He's trying to make up for lost time, as he babbles at me.

Hardly anyone can understand what he says just yet, so we all just nod in what we think are the appropriate spots. As he's talking my ear off, the guys show up with the dogs, as well as what appears to be our entire volunteer group.

Tucker grins as he walks over to me. "That looks good on you."

"This suit? I know." I look down at the one-piece with the sides cut out. "I don't wear it often, but I love it."

"No, I mean holding him." He nods at Keegan.

Before I can ask him what he means, Ransom yells, requesting help with the dogs. Instead of questioning him, I put that question in my back pocket for later.

CHAPTER THIRTY

Tucker

WALKING over to where Ransom stands with the dogs, I am slightly freaking out. Did I really just say that to Karsyn? Yeah, I decide, I did really just say that Karsyn. The next thing I ask myself, is did I mean it?

It takes me all of fifteen seconds to realize I meant it.

Now that I've learned more about her, about the fact she may have possibly never been around for me to get to know, I'm beginning to understand how much I need her in my life. Not only that, but I'm beginning to understand how much she adds to my life.

"We need to take them over there." Ransom points to the spot they've decided to hold the dog photos at. "Dad and Mason are going to be heading up this part."

"Gotcha." I grab Major's leash.

"Hey." Ransom stops me. "You okay? You look like you've either seen a ghost or like you're about to pass out."

Glancing back over at Karsyn, I see she's still holding

Keegan. That same feeling swamps me again. "Nah, I'm cool."

He looks over to where I was. "Oh I get it," he chuckles.

"You get what?" Now he's just irritating me.

"That first time you see your girl hold a baby, it makes you think shit. Shit you never thought you'd be thinking about. It's confusing, like you're all, I'm not ready for this, and the other part of you is like let's go fuck now."

I seriously hate when Ransom reads me so well. I'm not even sure how he got to be one of the people who reads me as well as he does. "Maybe."

"So that's all you're gonna say about it?" He shakes his head. "You got it bad my man."

"I don't have anything."

"Yes you do, and it's called settle-downitis, next will be baby fever."

"Stop it."

"Dude, you should just let it happen. Like now that you've started thinking about it, it's not going to go away. Trust me, I know this."

We're waiting for Ryan and Mason to get here, so I turn to face him. "It won't?"

"Nope." He leans down, giving Rambo a treat. He hands me one for Major and I do the same. "Once you get to that point, like you know she's the one for you? You know you're not going to let her go, there's no other woman for you. It's almost like everything reminds you of what you can have with her. Whether that be a kid, a life, whatever. It won't stop until you decide what you want to do."

If there's anything I know about Ransom, it's he's not shitting me. Out of everyone I know, Ransom has always been completely honest. So I guess the ball lies in my court. What do I want to do about the situation I find myself in?

"I KNOW you're about to welcome everybody here, but come with me for a sec." I grab Karsyn's hand, dragging her behind one of the buildings in this area.

"Tucker, what are you doing?" She laughs as she follows behind me."

"Just getting a few minutes alone with you before the craziness starts." I push her up against the wall, letting my gaze take her in. "I really like this bathing suit."

It has cut outs on the side, which show just enough skin to make me want to see what's underneath. The top cups her tits, pushing them slightly over the top of the suit, and her legs? I don't get to see them nearly enough. They're strong, slightly muscular and I find myself wishing I could reach down, grab those thighs, spread them, and have a few moments alone with her.

"I like it too." She grins, tilting her head to the side. "Kinda love what you're wearing." She hooks her fingers into the waistband of my shorts, pulling on them slightly.

"Wore it for you." I grin back at her.

She leans in, capturing my lips with hers. It's not often Karsyn takes the upper hand in anything we do, but I enjoy it no matter what. When she pulls back, we're both breathing a little harder.

"Proud of you." I push my hands into her hair. "You organized this all on your own, and you got everybody here today."

"Not on my own," she argues.

"Yes you did, I didn't do much at all."

"You've done all the heavy lifting."

"But this? It was your idea, and I know you. It scares you to come up with ideas, and say them in the presence of others."

"That has been a fear of mine, but when you broke my heart," she raises her eyebrows at me, "I decided I was done with waiting for things to happen. I made a deal with myself that I would do my best to do things I wanted to, instead of waiting for others to realize I wanted to do them. As much as it hurt for you to break up with me," she pulls bottom lip between her teeth before blowing out a deep breath, "it was needed. I had to grow up, and I never would have grown up. I would've always expected you to make things better for me. And that wasn't fair to you. It wasn't fair to me either, but it really wasn't to you. You deserve a woman who knows her own mind, who isn't easily swayed by others. Before I wasn't like that, and it wasn't because I didn't know my own mind, it was just I wasn't confident."

"You're right." I grab her hands, entwining our fingers together. "You weren't confident, and that's why I could run all over you back then. You should still tell me I'm a dick."

She giggles. "What would it help if I called you a dick now? I called you plenty of names back then, Tucker. Don't think all I did was cry. There were some voodoo dolls, not even kidding."

"I knew you were evil." I pull her hands hard, so that she stumbles into me. "But whatever it took, I'm glad we're back together."

"Me too." She tilts her head up to kiss me.

"We should get you back out to your adoring public," I joke when we break apart.

"I definitely think you're the one who will have an adoring public today."

I CAN'T EVEN BEGIN to explain how proud I am of Karsyn when she stands in front of everyone, waiting to get their attention. Some of them stopped talking as soon as she got up on the chair. Others are still having their own conversations, so I whistle loudly. She mouths a *thank you* to me.

"I just wanted to take a minute to thank everyone for coming. I know it's hot today, and if you're like me, you have a to-do list a mile long. The fact you've taken personal time out of your day to come and help us means so much. It won't be forgotten and you have our eternal thanks."

The group claps at the appropriate time.

"A few things, and then we'll be able to start letting people in. Whitney is doing childcare over there under the canopy." She points to where Whitney's standing with the kids she's already got for the day. "She also has some drinks and snacks. Leigh's graciously opened The Café to us if you want an actual meal. Just tell her you're with us, and it'll be free. Also, after we close for the day, they're feeding us, so stick around! The goal for today is at least ten thousand dollars, so we're hopeful to get enough for at least one dog."

There's another round of applause, and I slightly feel like I'm part of a football team who is getting a talking to by their coach before they go play in the big game.

"Those of you running the photo booth, please only allow people to take one picture. If that gets backed up, we'll never get them out of here."

She looks around at the group one more time, before she claps her hands.

"I'm pretty sure that's it. If you have a problem, please come and let me know. We're hoping not to have a huge back up on the street, but that seems inevitable. We'll deal with it as things happen. I'll be around everywhere, and we have four teams of volunteers as well as members of LSERT washing cars. Please wear your sunscreen, and if you get too hot, we have Cutter representing the EMT's and he'll help you cool down."

Cutter raises his hand to let the volunteers know who he is.

"Other than that, let's just have a great time and raise money for these dogs. Rambo and Major need a few days off," she jokes. Again, thank you all so much for being here. We honestly couldn't do it without all of you."

She hops down from the chair. I watch her and the Harrison family head to the entrance, taking the rope down, allowing our first group to come in. Glancing down the road, I can already see them lined up, and I can't help but be proud of what we've all come together to do.

Being a part of a family this big is one of the things I never expected, but I'm thankful it happened to me.

Laurel Springs takes care of its own, and I'm beyond grateful for being one of the people who call this amazing town my home.

CHAPTER THIRTY-ONE

Karsyn

TAKING a look at the line to get into the parking lot where we're washing cars, and I mean we're washing them, I'm so fucking proud. It travels at least a mile down the road. Other members of the Laurel Springs Police are directing traffic around it. There's also a few people taking donations only. In my wildest dreams, I couldn't have imagined this would be happening.

"This is amazing." Kels wraps her arm around my shoulder as we take a bit of a break. "I know, I'm going to go over and ask Mom if she has a preliminary count of how much we've raised. We've still got two hours to go, but I'm unsure if we'll be able to get all these cars done." I point to the line waiting to get in.

"We'll figure it out," she promises. "I'm gonna get back over there to where my hot-ass hubby is working hard with no shirt on." She purses her lips, making a noise in her throat.

"You do that," I laugh.

"Girl, I am on it." She wiggles her eyebrows.

I have a feeling she'll be on more than the situation at hand if given a few hours alone with Nick. Putting a shirt on over my bathing suit, because I feel my shoulders getting a little burnt, I walk over to where my mom is taking money. She's cute as hell wearing a shirt with Major on it, and a money belt.

"Hey, Mama," I greet her. "You need water or anything?"

"Nah, I'm fine. Tucker's been over here twice, telling me to hydrate and bringing me liters of water." She points to the empty bottles at her feet. "He's such a good guy," she sighs.

"I know, I have a feeling if given the chance, everyone would be half in love with him."

I look over to where him, Ransom, and Nick are working on a car. It's all status quo until it seems like Ransom says something to Tucker, which causes him to throw his sponge at Ransom, which accidentally hits Nick.

"Oh, it's on!"

Nick takes the water hose he's been in charge of and sprays them both. Before we know it, they're in a full-on water fight. I turn back to my mom. "They'll never grow up."

"No," she agrees. "They won't."

"So, do you have any kind of idea how much money we've raised?"

She looks down at her money belt. "Every thousand dollars I get, I've been giving it to Whitney." She points over to where Stella's mom is wrangling the kids. "She's got a lockbox over there."

"Sounds great!"

I'm realizing I didn't think anything about how this part

would go, and I'm so thankful that it seems like Whitney or Stella thought about it.

"I've gone over there at least eight times so far." Mom grins.

"Oh my God!" I wrap her up in a big hug. "We might hit our goal today!"

"Pretty sure we're gonna do more than hit our goal."

I'm so excited and proud, I have to turn away from her so she can't see the tears in my eyes. "Thank you for helping." I turn back to her, hugging her to my side.

"We wouldn't be anywhere else than here helping you, Karsyn. I hope you know that."

"I do."

Not wanting to take her attention away from her job anymore, I walk over to where Whitney is taking care of the kids. "How's it going?"

"Good!"

"It's so cool over here." I'm thankful as I step underneath the canopy she's set up.

"Yeah, there was no way I'd be able to stand out in this heat, and I didn't want the kids to get too hot either."

"So many of you thought of things I never did. I can't thank you enough for all the help you've given us."

She smiles softly. "I have a lot of experience making sure things are running the way they're supposed to be, and let's be honest, this helps my family as much as yours. We fight as one, Karsyn."

The slogan brings tears to my eyes again. "I'm beginning to understand those words more and more by the day."

Grabbing some water and some snacks, I walk over to where the Harrison family is dutifully directing people into the parking lot. "Brought you all some snacks and water!"

"I'm dying." Molly grabs the water, while Levi grabs the snack.

Caleb rolls his eyes. "It's not that freakin' bad, but I have to direct you to the line." He points up the road. "My mother is walking up that line taking donations," he laughs.

"Oh my God! When did she get here?"

"About an hour ago. She said people were just sitting there with nothing to do, so we may as well ask."

I notice the line is slightly smaller. "Karsyn," Karina yells at me, waving her arms. "I need help."

Quickly I jog up to where she's standing. "What's up?"

"I'm putting this money in my bra like a damn stripper. I need a money belt or something."

I giggle loudly at her words.

"No seriously." She leans over, showing me the money in her shirt.

"Holy hell woman!"

"People love the dogs and my son, I mean look at those three cuties!"

"I'll be right back."

As I hurry over to where I know we have something she may use to hold her money, I can't help but be so proud of these people and this town. This is more than I ever imagined it could be, and it's because of the family we've all scraped together.

IT'S hours later and we're in The Café. Leigh was beyond generous, offering to have us all in for a donated dinner. There's a huge group of us, and it's loud and boisterous. There's kids, dogs, adults - we're all here. My parents have been pulled into the middle of the Laurel Springs fold, something I'm pretty sure they've missed for how long we've lived here. Maybe that's my fault because they didn't want to give anyone a chance to see me. For a long time, even in this area, people knew about what happened to me, and always questioned me.

I'm sitting next to Tucker, his arm is around me, and we're laughing over something Ransom has just said when Mason whistles loudly.

"If I could have everyone's attention. I want to thank every single one of you for coming out today to help us and the counties surrounding us. You'll never know how much we appreciate it. There just wasn't enough money in our budgets to even think about getting another dog. It's something we've needed desperately, but without a fundraiser, we knew wouldn't be able to do it." He nods to me. "Enter Karsyn. Stand up, so those of you who may not know who are you can see you."

When I stand, Tucker whistles loudly, clapping.

My face burns bright red, even redder than the sun made it today. The crew all follows his lead, clapping for me. "Tucker helped me," I yell.

"The fuck he did." Nick's voice can be heard.

"Children are present!" someone else yells.

"Sorry, but we all know what he did was minimal."

"Either way, what you did and what he did is between the two of you." Mason nods to the both of us. "I'm glad to announce we've raised enough money today to get three dogs."

The noise in the room is deafening as some of the guys even bang on tables. I'm so proud as I watch everyone celebrating our win.

"We have an odd amount left, and with Karsyn and Tucker's blessing, we'd like to put that into a community fund."

"That's a great idea," I agree.

"We'll come up with an idea of what to use the community fund for, but I think we all agree that there are members of this town who need a little help from time to time."

Tucker wraps his arms around me from behind when I have a seat again. "I'm so proud of you," he whispers in my ear.

"I'm proud of you too, I wouldn't have done this if it hadn't been for you."

"Just to show me up." He nuzzles my neck.

"We were going to be together either way," I remind him. "Because this," I gesture between us, "was kinda meant to be, I think."

"I think you're right." He leans in, kissing me quickly. "We just had to get over ourselves."

"Over ourselves," I gasp. "You were the one who was all like, 'I can't have super real feelings for you, because I don't know what to do with myself'. You had to get over yourself." I point at him.

"Maybe." He shifts.

"Maybe my ass. It was all you, Tucker!"

"She's got you there," Nick chimes in.

Tucker turns on him. "You of all people have zero room to talk about me."

"Um, excuse you." He holds up his left hand. "Between us, who's married with kids and shit? Don't worry, I'll wait for you to figure it out."

"When did you become such a smartass?" Tucker groans as he faces away from Nick.

"Turn your back from the truth, it's okay."

"Do you hear someone speaking?" Tucker asks.

"Aww, poor thing, leave him alone Nick." I wrap him up in my arms. "The truth is sometimes too hard to accept."

"Oh my God," Tucker pulls back. "You too? I'm gonna go sit with people who like me. Come on, Major." He taps his leg.

When Major just looks at him and then gets up in the seat Tucker just vacated, everyone has a laugh at his expense.

CHAPTER THIRTY-TWO

Tucker

KARSYN and I are lying in bed, watching some show on Netflix, but I don't think either one of us are paying much attention to it.

"I can't believe how today went." She turns over onto her side, propping up on her arm. "Like I knew it was going to be okay, but I had no idea how good it would feel to plan that and have it work out," she grins.

"Like I told you, you should be confident. You're legit, Karsyn."

"Maybe I should apply to be Ruby's assistant." She laughs.

"I'm sure Caleb would appreciate that; it would give them more time together."

Reaching over, I push my fingers through her hair. "You're like glowing with accomplishment. I love this look on you. Honestly, there's nothing in the world I wouldn't do to give you this look all the time.'

Her eyes flit down my body, then back up to my eyes. "Really?"

I'm not sure where she's going with this, but it's safe to say I'm on board with whatever she wants to do. "Yeah, if you could see yourself, you're so proud of yourself."

"I am," she agrees. "I guess I just never realized how much I sometimes need that affirmation."

"I'd give it to you any day of the week, babe. Don't even think I won't."

"So." She quirks her lips. "Would you let me do something I've kinda wanted to do a while? It's one of those things I've wanted to do, but have been slightly shy about."

"You can do whatever you want to, you don't even have to ask. Just assume it's a yes."

She giggles loudly before getting up and walking over to shut the door. "Don't want a repeat of what happened to Ransom." She winks.

I laugh, thinking about him being so offended by a dog nose in the ass. It makes my heart beat slightly faster too, because that might mean we're about to get naked together. I promise myself though that I won't pressure her, I won't try to speed her up. This goes at her pace.

My gaze follows her as she resumes her spot beside me, propping her head up again on her hand. I'm tense, waiting to see what she's going to do. I don't think I've ever been this tense before.

Her hand starts in the middle of my stomach, making my abs clench. She runs it slowly to the waistband of the basketball shorts I'm wearing. Ducking underneath them, she continues her slow slide down into my boxer briefs. A noise escapes the back of my throat as she wraps her hand around my length. I'm hot, hard, and ready for this in less than five seconds. I don't know what it is about her putting her hands on me, but I am so fucking ready.

"Just relax," she whispers in my ear. For some reason I kind of feel like I should be the one telling her those words.

Tilting my head back against my pillow, I watch her through hooded eyes. The way my shorts move with the way her hand jacks me. There's something about not being able to see it, but definitely being able to feel it.

"I can't believe how quickly you got hard for me."

A strangled laugh accompanies my words. "It doesn't take much, Syn. A look, a promise, a whisper on your lips. Any of those things make me hard for you. Sometimes it doesn't even take that, just being with you is enough. Because I know what you look like when I'm going down on you, right at that moment when I enter you. It's all enough."

"Tucker, do you ever touch yourself?" she asks softly. But she doesn't wait for me to answer before she keeps talking. "Because I do. Sometimes when I need to relax, or I'm waiting for you to get home from a long shift. I lay here, thinking about the things you've done to me. Maybe something that really got me excited, and I just can't help it."

Jesus fucking Christ, this woman. "What are some of the things you think about?"

It's not going to help me keep my erection for long. I'm positive I'm only a few minutes from coming, but it's not often Karsyn's this honest with me. Usually she's shy and embarrassed. I'm not sure what's come over her tonight, but I want this part of her. I need to hear what she does when I'm not around. It's either this or fucking die.

"The look on your face you have right now." She speaks directly into my ear. "Your eyes are hooded, jaw is slack, and it looks like you're on the best ride of your life. This is how I love to think about you, and it gets me wet," she answers.

"Does it?" I question. I need to know the answer, like needed to know it five minutes ago.

A noise of disappointment leaves me as she drops my cock, but I watch her, curious as to what she's going to do. Holy shit, she puts the hand she was using to stroke me in between her legs, past her panties, and strokes herself for a few seconds. When she's done, she takes that same hand and puts it back on my cock. I can feel it, soaking wet, slick and everything I enjoy about getting or receiving a hand job.

"Fuck you're wet."

"Told you," she giggles.

"What else do you like to think about?"

I need to know all the things, I want to make all her dreams come true, and honestly, I'm not sure when she'll ever be like this again. I have to take advantage of it now that I have her unguarded, her barriers down.

"The way your stomach tightens, your thighs too. Sometimes you get goosebumps across your skin. It's times like that, when I know I've got you right where I want you. Lift up your hips," she directs.

And finally she takes me out of my clothes, which gives me some room to breathe and does nothing to diminish my erection. Now she can move her hand easier, from root to tip. Stroking me up and down. This is the shit dreams are made of, and I swear I'm not going to do anything to stop it.

"The way you make those noises in the back of your throat. I wish you'd make those noises all the time, but you don't."

"Because as a teenager, you're programmed to be quiet,

don't want your mom to walk in while you're beating one off," I answer in between heaving breaths.

"That's kinda what I like about getting myself off." She nips at my throat. "I'm not self-conscious about how loud I am, I don't worry that I look like an idiot. It's just for me. Nobody else."

"Fuck." I run my hands through my short hair. "I'd love for it to be for me. Jesus Christ, I wish you'd do it for me. Ten seconds flat I'd be blowing my load."

The voice that comes out of her isn't one I've ever heard before, and it's damn sexy. "Maybe, just maybe, you'll get lucky in a few minutes."

"God I hope so. Take your clothes off for me," I whisper.

She stops her ministrations, standing up to do exactly what I've asked her to do. This time instead of lying next to me, though, she straddles me. Grabbing her around the waist, I hold on tight, not sure what she's going to do.

When she grabs hold of my cock, I punch my head back against the pillow. Instead of putting it into her pussy, she presses it down against my stomach, and when she starts sliding against it, I can't help what comes out of my mouth. "Fucking shit, don't stop."

Her pussy is wet and the way she's using it to jack me off is enough to blow my mind. She's warm, wet, and the rate she moves this way is faster than her hand earlier. She moans. "Am I hitting your clit?"

"Yes." She tosses her head back. The ends of it brush against my thighs and even that causes me to shiver.

"C'mon," I encourage her. "Get yourself and me off together. I wanna see you lose control."

Her hands balance against my pecs as she rocks up and down, slides back and forth. We're both sweating, her nails curl, trying to gain purchase on my skin. When she does, I hold onto her hands, helping her maintain her position.

"Feels so good." She moves in such a way her tits bounce up and down before swinging back and forth.

"It does, it feels fucking fantastic. Don't stop, whatever you do, don't stop," I want her to keep going. "Whatever it takes for you to get off, don't be scared, don't be shy. Take what you want, what you need. You get off, I'll get off."

She moves with abandon, doing exactly what I've asked her to do. Karsyn gets wetter, making noises deep in her throat. Those same noises she liked me making, I like her making too.

"Oh, oh, oh." Her body convulses, pitching forward against me, right as I feel myself come too. I'm saying all kinds of shit, have no idea what's actually coming out of my mouth, but as she stops shaking, and I can finally open my eyes, I know this has been another turning point for us.

With my arms wrapped tightly around her, I know I'm never going to let this woman go.

CHAPTER THIRTY-THREE

Karsyn

"HEY!" I smack Tucker's hand when he reaches in, stealing a piece of my bacon. "I offered to make you breakfast, and you were all, I'll just have a protein shake. Which means you don't get bacon."

He doesn't drop it. Instead, he stands in front of me, making a big show out of eating it.

"Go ahead, enjoy it, I'll never cook bacon for you, ever."

He finishes eating it before he has a seat across from me at his kitchen table. Major's outside getting his morning business in. "C'mon." He chucks me under the chin. "You know you'll cook for me. You can't help but want to take care of me."

I frown, because he's got me there. He knows me probably better than I know myself when it comes to what I will do for him. Not giving him exactly what he wants, I raise an eyebrow. "I might cook it for you, but I'll burn it to hell."

A laugh works its way past his throat and a smile spreads across his face. "I'd expect nothing less from you, Syn."

"Don't call me that cute nickname and think that's gonna change things, Tuck."

"Touché," he chuckles again.

Neither one of us talk. He drinks his coffee, I drink my orange juice. We're eyeing each other over our respective cups. Reaching over, he takes mine out of my hands, before standing up and coming to where I sit. When he does, he pulls me up to him. I have to stand on my tiptoes to be able to put my arms around his neck, but I manage.

"What are you doing, Officer Williams?"

He smirks when I call him Officer.

"Trying to send my girl off with a smile to work, but you're making it difficult."

"Am I?" I unhook my arms, putting my palms on the sides of his neck.

"Slightly." He raises an eyebrow. "But whatever, I'll still send you off with a smile."

"Oh, will you?"

"You can bet your ass." His arms around my waist move down to my ass, where he palms them, pulling me in closer.

Before I can open my mouth, he's claimed it, grabbing my flesh in his hands, squeezing tightly. It's almost as if he's directing my mouth by the way he's gripping my skin, then letting it go.

When he pulls his mouth from mine, the world spins slightly and it takes me a moment to get my equilibrium back. He holds me, grinning. "You okay?"

"You literally made the room spin for me. That should send you off with a smile on your face."

"It does."

Glancing over to the clock above the sink, I feel a rush to my system. "Is that clock right?" I point to it.

"Yeah, it's actually five minutes slow."

"Oh shit." I immediately disentangle myself from him. "I have to be at work in twenty minutes, and it'll take me at least thirty to get there."

"If I were you, I'd suggest not speeding. I'd hate to see you get a ticket."

"Oh my God, you're such an asshole." I throw a muffin at his head. "I can't believe you'd bring that up right now."

He ducks with a shit-eating grin on his face. "It's what brought you to me. To this day you're still my favorite traffic stop."

"I damn well better be."

Racing to his bedroom, I finish dressing, putting my earrings in as I run back into the kitchen.

"I made you something." He holds out a brown paper bag to me. "It's not much."

My heart warms, knowing he's taken a few moments out of his super busy morning to do something nice for me. "Is this lunch?"

"Whenever you wanna eat it." He shrugs. "It's just a peanut butter and jelly sandwich with some chips and cookies."

"What kind of peanut butter and jelly?"

"Crunchy peanut butter, strawberry jelly on white."

"And the chips?"

"Funyuns. I put a breath mint in there too, because I know you're self-conscious about it."

I'm feeling lucky to know he's remembered all of this about me. For some reason I need to know he remembers the rest. "What about the cookies?"

"Oreo. Duh? Is there any other kind?"

I throw my arms around him, hugging tightly. "I never realized you knew this much about me."

He seems to want to act like this isn't that big of a deal, but it is. It's a huge deal. A year ago, we wouldn't be doing this. A year ago I wouldn't even be here at his house, much less spending the night. "I spend a lot of time with you," he says like it's not a big thing. "I've learned stuff about you because you're a creature of habit. There's nothing wrong with that."

"No there's not," I agree.

I became a creature of habit because change gave me and still gives me anxiety. I like to know where I'm going, what I'm doing and who will be there with me. It obviously even extends into the foods I eat and the drinks I drink.

"I gotta go." I stand on my tiptoes, kissing him softly.

"Have a good day." He puts his forehead to mine. "I love you."

The side of my mouth hitches up, I never thought I'd hear him say those words so easily. Much less with so much conviction. "I love you too. Be safe out there today."

"We will be."

Major barks from where he sits at my feet. "Don't think I forgot you." I lean down, rubbing his face and neck. He reaches up, giving me doggy kisses. "You be good too," I tell him. "Catch a whole bunch of bad guys." He barks like he knows what I've told him to do.

Before I walk out the door, I turn back to wave at them.

IF ANYONE TOLD me to describe my perfect morning, it

would have been this one, I think as I drive to work. It's true that I never thought I would be able to have this kind of morning with Tucker, but he's surprising me at every turn.

I'm late as I pull into the parking lot, but there aren't many cars here yet, which means we don't have many patients. I hope this day is an easy one. All I want to do is get back home to my boys. Maybe tonight I'll pretend we're like a real married couple or something, and make him dinner.

Walking into the building, I'm surprised when I see everybody crowded around the television.

"What's going on?"

Immediately I'm concerned there's been another mass shooting or something of that nature. I'm totally unprepared for what I see.

"Breaking News. Clarence Night who is serving a forty-five-year sentence for kidnapping, among other things, has escaped from the Birmingham Federal Corrections Complex. All we know so far is he had a medical emergency and was supposed to be transferred to a medical facility. The ambulance picked him up with no issue, but between the drive from Birmingham Federal Corrections and the hospital, there was an altercation. During the altercation, Clarence Night escaped."

In my head I can hear them saying what he looks like, repeating his previous crimes, and telling the public to consider him armed and dangerous. My phone rings, and when I look down I see Shelby's name.

"Hello," I answer it without a thought.

"I take it you've seen the news, given the tone of your voice." She doesn't even say who she is.

"I saw it."

"The prison called me, to get in touch with you. They

don't know if he'll come for you again, Karsyn, but it's a possibility. You did put him away, and you kept him in jail. None of us know where his head is right now."

"What should I do?"

Immediately I'm taken back to that young girl I was. I'm shaking as I listen to her give me instructions. I'm to go to the police station, and I can't even begin to comprehend how happy I am to go there. There I'll not only have my person, but my dog too.

"Okay," I answer. "I'm gonna head that way right now."

"I really wish you'd let me get you an escort, Karsyn," she argues.

For some reason this is the thing that breaks the camel's back. Maybe because I've been living my life without anyone telling me what to do for a while now, maybe it's because I've gotten used to not looking over my shoulder. Whatever it is, I don't appreciate her wanting me to have an escort.

"I can do this on my own," I bite into the phone. "I don't need an escort to get to the police station."

"At least let us follow you," Kels is saying, wringing her hands in front of her.

"Yes, at least let them follow you. I know you care so much for your independence, Karsyn, but this is a matter of public safety."

Sighing, I consent before hanging up. Honestly what they're saying is true. I shouldn't be arguing with them. If I get hurt, it doesn't do anything for anyone. It takes away precious resources that can be used to find him.

Getting into my car, I do my best to push the tears back. How did such a happy ride a few minutes ago, turn into this? I hate this with everything in me, and as I pull into the police station lot, I can't help but let some of those tears fall.

CHAPTER THIRTY-FOUR

Tucker

"DOES anyone have any idea why we were called in for this meeting?"

Ransom, Caleb, and Nick sit in the front row of our common meeting room. There'd been no information given to me, just an emergency response to get to this space at a certain time.

"Negative, Ghostrider," Ransom answers.

"Do you really have to quote *Top Gun*?" I grimace. "It's not my favorite."

"Nobody asked you, Tucker." He folds his arms over his chest.

Just as I'm about to tell him what I think about him asking me, Mason walks into the room.

It doesn't take long for us to realize something serious has happened. He immediately goes to the front and waits for the room to settle. All I have to do is look at this face and I snap to attention.

When some of the room keeps on talking, he gets irritated. He whistles before yelling. "Settle down."

The group of us who've gathered know that tone. It's one that means he's not playing around. Looking around the room, he makes sure to meet every single one of our eyes. He's good about that. Letting us know the severity of the situation before he even begins.

Papers are shuffled before he begins speaking.

"An hour ago Clarence Night," I shiver when I hear that name, "told prison officials he thought he was having a heart attack. They treated him at the prison but knew he'd have to be transferred to a hospital. The facility doesn't have the proper equipment to accurately assess if a patient is indeed having a cardiac event. The one thing they did know was his heart-rate was slow."

My stomach drops, something about this doesn't sit well with me, even before we know what it is.

"In transport, there was an altercation in the ambulance, and Clarence escaped."

Son of a bitch.

"Care to explain to me what the fuck altercation means?" I ask before I can convince myself it's not the right question to ask. My tone is this side of disrespectful, but I can't help it.

"First, you can take the attitude down a notch. Second, there were two EMT's in there with him. Male and female. The male was driving and the female was administering treatment. She was stabbed with a shank in the stomach, he had his throat slit with the same shank."

I tilt my head back, doing my best to take a deep breath. "Are they alive?" I realize as soon as I ask the question, I don't really want to know the answer, but now that I've opened this can of worms, there's no putting it back.

Mason looks like he doesn't want to tell us what the outcome is, which is unusual because he's always been honest with us.

"Neither one of them made it."

Now I want to rage. Every single part of my body wants to go into the workout room and beat the fuck out of a bag. I want to rapidly lift weight and run a mile in five minutes, empty my clip into some fucker who doesn't deserve to live. None of this makes sense.

"How did he get out of the ambulance?" Caleb asks the other question I had, but couldn't seem to form.

"They ran into extremely heavy traffic. They were forced to stop because of construction. He had time to put the EMT uniform on. He parked the ambulance and made like he was going in to let them know they had arrived. When the back of the ambulance was opened, what they found were the two deceased EMT's."

Such a fucking waste. All of this is. People like this always find a way to circumvent the rules, and now I'm even angrier than I started out being.

"Do we have any idea where he's going?" Nick asks.

"No." Mason crosses his arms over his chest. "We've contacted the FBI and the Tennessee Highway Patrol. They were the ones who headed up the original investigation. Right now we're waiting."

"I can't wait." I stand up. "We've got to get out there and start looking. They have to have something with his scent on it. Major and me, along with Ransom and Rambo could start tracking. Maybe we could find him before he hurts someone else."

"That's what I was going to suggest." He flips through his notes. "Goes without saying overtime is approved for everyone. We're not leaving until we get this guy."

He looks at me, motioning me over. "Karsyn's here and we need to talk to her," he says the words quietly. "Do you want to be in on this or not. Obviously she's not in trouble, but maybe she can give us something to work with. She's the only one who knows what happened the last time he was running from the cops."

I don't want to do this, no part of me wants to do it, but I know I need to be there for her. If I'm not here for her right now, I'll never forgive myself and neither will she.

SHE LOOKS SO small sitting in the interrogation room. They've at least not made it like a freezer in here for her.

"Hey, babe," I grab her up in my arms when she stands.

"Hey." She wraps her arms tightly around me. "Is it true?"

"Yeah, looks like it."

Mason sits down, motioning for both of us to do the same. "I hate to be the person asking you these questions, Karsyn, but it's important."

"I know." She grabs hold of my hand. "I don't know what I can do to help, but I know I want to."

"Tell me." Mason scoots in, making a note on his piece of paper. "What was his plan after he took you? Did he have one?"

She's slow to answer, like she's doing her best to think back to that time in her life. Truth is, if someone were coming at me like this, I'd be slow to answer too, but probably out of fucking spite.

"There are a lot of stupid things I remember about those couple of days." She swallows loudly. "But there's a few things that stick out. He had a map. It wasn't like a GPS, or a phone. It was a paper map, and he had a route drawn on it, along with different ways he could take if one wasn't available to him."

So the fucker had planned it down to his route. This pisses me off more than it probably should.

"When he took you, did he stop to get the clothes for you to change into? Or maybe the dye to dye your hair?"

She thinks back, that far-off look is on her face again. "No." She shakes her head. "He had like a go bag in the trunk with most of what he would need. I don't recall us ever stopping for anything other than gas and food."

Mason makes a note, looking at me. "He's got to have someone on the outside, he's got to have stashed something either with someone or someone has stashed it somewhere."

"I agree, we need to get a perimeter, like how far could he have gone from where the hospital in the amount of time it took them to get patrol cars in there. We also need to see if there've been any reports of any other crimes that he could be responsible for. That'll help us."

"Anything else you can give us that might help?" I ask Karsyn, rubbing her neck.

"I'm trying to think." Her tone is pleading. "There were so many things he did I thought were weird." She runs her hands through her hair.

"But is there one thing? One thing that separates him from other people besides that damn tattoo he has?"

She looks me dead in the eyes. "He likes girls, Tucker.

There's gonna be another one. He's been in jail for how long? There's gonna be another one, and I have an idea she's going to look like me when I was young."

I know she's right, but I don't want to believe it. More than anything I want to believe we can protect everyone in our jurisdiction.

"He's gonna go where he can get a girl," I tell Mason. "Where he can get one easily."

The group of us move to the meeting room we were in earlier. He's gotten everyone together, along with a few of our IT guys. "I want a map of the area around the hospital. Is there a school? What about a playground?"

"There's both," he tells us.

"We need to lock that school down, and get the kids off the playground," I speak the obvious.

"Let's just hope we've gotten to it fast enough," Ace says from where he stands.

"What should we do?" Caleb asks. "Get down there?"

Mason looks at his son. "We haul ass and start tracking. The dogs are going to be the only thing that'll be able to track him, because once he changed those clothes, we're already behind him."

I'm in my SUV traveling at over one-hundred-miles-per-hour toward Birmingham when the Amber Alert comes over the radio. We aren't in time. As they were taking head-count at the elementary school they realized a little girl went to recess and didn't come back.

Clarence Night has kidnapped his second child. Right under our noses, and I don't know about anybody else, but I have a feeling blood will be shed this time, and it won't be mine.

CHAPTER THIRTY-FIVE

Karsyn

I'M STILL SITTING in the police station when I hear the Amber Alert come out. My stomach drops to my knees, because I know what's coming for this girl. They say her name is Leah, and when they show her picture, I start shaking. She could be my twin when I was a little girl.

Immediately I want to help. There's no way I can sit here in this room and not do anything. It goes so far against everything I've learned about myself, the person I've become. Getting up, I walk over to where Holden is sitting at the information desk. Even though he's officially retired, he volunteers a few hours a week here. He can't stand to do nothing from what I've heard.

"I wanna help," I tell him.

He nods solemnly. "Are you sure? This isn't easy, you may see things you won't ever be able to forget."

"I live with that every day," I remind him. "I was his first victim." But I think about that, and something tells me I'm not actually his first victim. "Scratch that, I'm the first one who got him caught. He may have had more before me, but I was smart enough to stay alive. Please," I beg him, "let me help this girl."

It's obvious he doesn't want to put me in harm's way, I can see it in his eyes, but at the same time he knows I'm right. He has an argument with himself, I can literally see it as it passes across his face.

"Shit." He throws a pen across the desk. "Grab your stuff, we're an hour behind everybody else."

Adrenaline fuels me, making me run across the room, quickly grabbing what I brought when they insisted I come here. Holden is already standing up, ready to leave when I come back out.

"I'm ready."

"Let's get going."

Both of us run out to the parking lot. He goes to a fast-looking Dodge Charger, I follow. As we get inside and buckled in, he looks over, grinning. "It's been a long time since I drove one of these, and I'd be lying if I said I'm not looking forward to this."

"It's definitely a nice piece of machinery." I inhale the smell of the leather seats and admire the dashboard. "I have one like this, but I bet mine can't do what yours can."

"You ever rode with a cop before?"

"Tucker's driven me around."

"No." He chuckles. "Like in a police car?"

"Oh." I shake my head. "No, haven't had the pleasure."

"There's an *oh shit* handle above you, feel free to grab it if you need to."

I don't even have a chance when he peels out of the parking lot, squealing tires. It's obvious he knows how to drive though, because even though my stomach is in my throat, his hands are firmly around the wheel, holding it securely.

"Trust me," he tells me as we get on the interstate. "I know how to drive; I can handle the speed, and I won't do anything that puts us in danger."

We hit the interstate, sirens blaring, and my eyes widen as I see the speedometer rise past a hundred miles an hour. I decide really quickly I don't want to watch this. Instead I grab my phone out of my purse and start reading up on what they know so far about Leah. It's research, I tell myself, not a sickening need to know what he's doing.

"I should have us down there in less than an hour."

"Got it," I whisper, fully engrossed on what's going on, and deciding this time, he won't get to keep this girl for as long as he kept me.

Tucker

"IF HE'S FOLLOWING his previous MO, he's got a hotel room somewhere," I mention to Caleb as we discuss where we can search next.

"But which one." He pulls up a Google Map. "There's legit a hundred around here."

"Okay." Nick comes into the conversation. "Let's think about this. He's been in jail for fourteen years. He doesn't have a credit card. He doesn't know about chips in debit cards. What he was able to get on work detail, or through prison is probably cash."

"We need a seedy motel." I'm thinking as I start

narrowing down the options by excluding places that would need a credit card.

"He's not got an ID either," Caleb reminds us. "If he does, it isn't his. It's one of those EMT's, so we need to get their names."

"Okay." I tap on the tablet we're using. "There are five motels in the area that are legit motels. I'm talkin' these are probably rented by the hour. We need to get these checked out."

We're convening with the Birmingham police as well as the FBI when I see one of our Chargers roll up to the scene. Karsyn gets out of the passenger seat, and immediately I'm on high-alert.

"What the fuck is she doing here?"

"Before you say anything," Holden stops me at the pass, "she wanted to come, and I think she's right. She's the only person who knows Clarence. I say let's give her a chance to help us. If it doesn't work out, then we haven't lost anything. Hopefully we've gained a whole hell of a lot."

Karsyn is standing next to him, those eyes of hers big as hell. "C'mere." I motion with my hand, pulling her back behind my SUV. "What the fuck are you thinking?"

"That I can help, Tucker. Please let me help. I know him, and I can't live with myself if something happens to this girl."

"This isn't your responsibility," I remind her.

"It is," she argues. "I owe it not only to her, but to the girl I was all those years ago. Nobody could help me. I can help her, please don't stand in my way."

"What are you going to do if I don't let you help?"

Her chin lifts in defiance, her eyes spark and fuck if it's not sexy as hell.

"I'll go above you." She folds her arms across her chest. "You're not the one in charge here. You may have a badge, but you don't have the authority to tell me if I can help or not."

She's got me there, and I know Mason; he'll let her help and he'll have her ride with someone else if she goes over my head. It's against my better judgement, but I relent.

"Let me go tell Mason you'll be with me, but first we lay down some ground rules."

"Okay." She nods.

"You do what I tell you to do, every time I tell you to do it. This is my job, it's my specialty and there are situations I won't allow you to be a part of."

"Got it."

"That's not it. You wear a vest. Anything can happen out there, and I want you as safe as possible."

"No question," she agrees.

I can't believe I'm doing this as I go tell Mason she's here and wants to help.

"Get her over here," he barks at me. "She may be able to tell us which motel he's more likely to be at."

Running back to my SUV, I reach in the back, grabbing out my extra vest. "Come here, Syn."

As I help her pull it on and secure it around her, I feel an unexpected rush of tears. Pushing them back, I use my index finger to tilt her face up to mine. "Thank you for doing this, but if you get hurt I'll never forgive myself."

"I'll be fine, Tuck. Just like you are."

She leans in, kissing me softly. I let her, but in the back of my mind, I know that everything isn't always fine, no matter what I tell her at the end of every shift. Some of them are worse than others. Some I'll never be able to forget. There are a few that still keep me up at night.

"I love you," I tell her, pulling her into a hug.

"I love you, too, and I promise to listen to everything you tell me. I don't want to distract you from doing your job and you end up getting hurt. All I want to do is help."

"Come on, Mason thinks you can help us pick which motel he might be at."

Hand in hand, we walk over to where everyone's crowded around the tablet we've been using.

"Hey, Karsyn, if you could help us, that would be great." Mason moves the tablet so she can see it. "These are all motels we think he may be at with Leah. Is there anything that stands out to you about any of them?"

She picks up the tablet, going through the pictures we've managed to collect of them and their surrounding areas. I watch her, her brows drawn together in concentration.

"Can I see more of these two." She points to honestly the two I would have ruled out.

Mason checks which ones she's pointed to, and then speaks to one of the IT people on scene. When they get more of them, he hands her the tablet back.

"This one." Her voice is confident.

"Want to tell me why?" Mason asks.

"Two things." She uses her fingers to zoom in on the one she's picked. "This one is a complete motor court. There aren't stairs. I don't know if he makes this known or whatever, but Clarence walks with a limp. It's very hard for him to climb stairs. And, I'm looking at the timestamps here." She points to a set of pictures. "There's a nondescript van in that parking spot now. Something tells me this is it."

CHAPTER THIRTY-SIX

Tucker

"RUN A REPORT ON THAT VAN," Mason yells. "Find out if the owner knows where it is, or better yet, find the damn owner."

We decide quickly that we're going to wait until we hear back from the owner. Birmingham police have already sent a unit over to the last known address. My heart is pounding as I stand with the rest of my fellow officers and Karsyn, waiting to hear if this van is stolen.

When our radios start squawking, my adrenaline spikes again.

Registered owner of the van say it's stolen. Repeat registered owner of the van is reporting it stolen.

That's all I need to hear. I grab Karsyn's hand and together we run for my SUV.

"What does this mean?" she asks as she buckles in. "It means he's probably right where you said he was gonna be."

"Shouldn't we wait for everyone else?"

"It was already discussed and decided that Ransom and I would take point on this. If he runs, we need to be there ASAP to get the dogs on the scent."

Major is whining and barking in his cage in the back. If I could will my SUV to move faster I would. My hands are shaking and sweating as I navigate the streets, following my on-board GPS. Ransom is hot on my tail as we speed through town. I have to give it to Karsyn, she's quietly holding on as we're jostled with every turn we take. We're approaching the motel, and just as we get eyes on it, I see something that makes my stomach turn.

"He's taking her out!" she screams, pointing to what's going on in front of us.

"Be advised, suspect is moving the girl. He's getting into the van right now," I tell everyone of the situation going down on the radio. "Permission to initiate chase?"

"You have to ask for that?" Karsyn yells.

I tap the mike off. "It's not my jurisdiction, Karsyn. We have to get permission."

A voice I've never heard comes over the radio. "Permission granted. Do what you have to in order to get her back."

"We'll need backup." I can hear Ransom over the radio.

"It's coming." We're promised.

I have a feeling it's not coming fast enough as the van squeals out of the parking lot. There are many times in this job when I wish I had wings to fly, or super human skills so I could stop bad things from happening. This is one of those times.

The atmosphere in the SUV is tense as we give chase. Ransom is calling out where we're going on his radio, because it's taking all I can to keep my SUV on the road. A summer thunderstorm has roared up onto us, and it's dropping rain in buckets.

"Fuck!" I punch the steering wheel. "If he gets out, this rain is going to make it harder to track him."

"Do you think he knew this?" Karsyn asks quietly. "Like did he have the perfect plan?"

"I don't know," I answer her honestly. "I'm not sure what he was given access to in prison as far as weather reports or anything of that nature. Could be he's just getting really lucky. One thing we do have over him," I nod as he almost loses control of the van, "is he hasn't driven like this in fourteen years. Sooner or later, he's gonna wreck out."

"At what cost?" she asks. "What if the girl is hurt?"

"Even if she's hurt, she won't be with him anymore. You were hurt from your wreck," I remind her. "But you were okay with it because you no longer had to be with him."

She's biting her nail in the passenger seat, and for what's it worth, I can understand where she's coming from. It doesn't make things any easier, knowing she's worried, but I'm doing what I have to do. This is the part of police work no one ever sees. The moments when we're forced to make decisions that have life-altering consequences. We make the best decisions we can, but sometimes they aren't perfect. Actually more often than not, someone can find fault with them.

"Shit," I curse as I watch him barely miss someone on the interstate. When he swerves to avoid hitting them, he hits a puddle of water.

We watch, both of us shouting, I'm not sure what we're shouting, but we are, as the van goes airborne, turning over and over, before coming to a stop in the grass.

"Stay in the car," I tell her as I get out.

I grab Major, and we approach.

"Get out of the van with your hands up!" I yell, authority in my voice.

Beside me Major is barking ferociously. There's no movement, and I approach as slowly as I can.

"Clarence Night, come out of the van with your hands up."

"Fuck you!"

So he's at least able to respond. "If you don't come out, I'm sending the dog in and you will be bit."

"Send him in, I'll take care of him," he yells.

The fuck he will.

Ransom comes up on the other side of the van. I can hear Rambo barking too.

"Gun!" Ransom yells.

And it's then I see him crawling out on his stomach. It happens so fast. He crawls just enough to give himself the stability to fire a shot. There's a double *pop pop* in the air as I release Major's leash, go down on one knee, and fire two shots in succession. It's a kill-shot and I know it as soon as I pull the trigger. There wasn't anything else for me to aim at other than his head.

My vest takes his shot, sending me flying backward with the force of impact. I hear Karsyn scream in the background. She must get out of the SUV because she's standing over me. "Tucker, are you okay?"

One thing most people don't know about vests is they hurt like hell when they catch a bullet. All that centrifugal force is stopped on a dime, and I took two of them. I'm struggling to catch my breath. To let her know I'm okay.

"He's fine." Ransom kneels next to me. "We need to get the vest off so he can take a breath. When he releases one side, Karsyn releases the other side. It's then that I can finally take a breath.

"Shit," I heave trying to get my bearings back. "The girl?"

"The EMT's are here," Ransom tells me.

I look over and she's being taken from the wreckage to the back of an ambulance, no doubt to be checked out.

"Clarence?"

"He's gone," Mason tells me as he walks over to me. "I need your gun."

This is standard operating procedure, and we know it, but it still sucks.

"Why is he taking your gun?" Karsyn looks between everyone.

"When you kill someone in the line of duty, they always have to do an investigation," Ransom explains to her. "But this was completely justified. He'll get a few days off with pay, and then be able to return back. It's normal."

She looks relieved. "Shouldn't you be checked out by the EMT'S too?"

"He should be," Nick says as he reaches down to help me up. "You could have some internal bruising."

"I'm tough." I try to act that way, but I have to bend over at the waist to try and get my breath.

"More than anyone, I know you are," Karsyn whispers in my ear. "But please get checked out. I don't know what I would do if something happened to you because of him."

We hold hands tightly as she helps me walk over to the ambulance.

THREE HOURS later we're getting an escort back to Laurel Springs. She's sitting in the backseat of a car with me, and I'm holding her tightly in my arms. "I'm so glad you're okay," she whispers, rubbing at the places where I have bruising.

"I'm glad you're okay," I whisper back. "My biggest fear was he was going to get out and get to you. I can only imagine what he thought of you. How much he blamed you for all the shit he's gone through. Of course I was worried about the girl too, but you're always my top priority, even when you maybe shouldn't be."

She reaches up, kissing me on the jawline.

"Where am I taking you?" Nick asks as we hit the Laurel Springs City Limits. "Your house or her apartment?"

Today has put a lot of things in perspective for me. One being that life can be taken away from you at any time. I'm not an idiot, I always knew that was the case, but there's something about being on the receiving end of two bullets - it makes you think about all the things you've been putting off.

"My house," I tell him. "Our house."

She looks at me, tears pooling in those dark eyes. "Are you sure?"

"I've wanted it for a while, but I didn't know how to tell you, or I put off telling you. Today taught me a lot."

"It taught me a lot, too."

When he pulls in, and we get out, we walk in as a family. Her, me, and Major. The family we've been for each other since she came into my life. Maybe I wasn't smart about it to begin with, but I'll be fucking damned if I let this gift go.

Not everybody is given second chances, and I promise myself I won't fuck this one up.

CHAPTER THIRTY-SEVEN

Karsyn

"HOW'S IT GOING?" Kels asks as I have a seat in the chair next to her.

She's updating her charts, which I've already done mine. "I want my peace back again," I grimace. "I've had to change my number again." I frown. "You should be getting a text from me tonight with my new one.

Since everything came out with Clarence, news organizations have found my name, and they're all asking for interviews about what happened not only recently, but back in my childhood. To say I'm sick of it is an understatement.

"It's a good thing you and Tucker moved in together, huh?"

"Yeah," I agree. "I went by my apartment yesterday because I have like a box of clothes left there. I can't tell you how many news vans were there. I just said fuck it, I'll buy new clothes. So far no one seems to know I've moved in with him."

"Today's a big day for him, isn't it?"

I grin. "It is. He should get the okay to go back to work. Not that I haven't loved having him off to help me move and get stuff set up, but he's starting to get cabin fever. So is Major. They're both slightly starting to get on my nerves."

"I feel ya. If Nick's home too long, him and D-man decide to do projects." She uses air quotes for the word. "Typically I have to hire someone to fix what they've messed up. I love them so much, but damn."

"So the news, is that why you're hanging out in the back?" She flips over her chart.

"Yeah, Dr. Patterson was scared for me to work the registration desk."

"Good call." She gives me a wink. "That means maybe you can go to The Café and get us lunch?"

"Ohh, it's chicken sandwich Thursday." I rub my stomach. "My favorite."

"So you can get us lunch?"

"Hell yeah, you want me to go now?" I look up at the clock, seeing it's almost eleven-thirty.

"Go." She hitches her head to the door. "I'll take care of it until you get back."

I'VE NEVER BEEN the type of person who thought I'd be attached to my car, but lately this is the only time I can get complete peace. Here, there aren't people trying to get my attention, trying to find things out about me that I don't want to share.

This is the one place during the day I can be myself.

Grabbing my cell phone, I call The Café, putting our order in, because I don't want to wait once I get there.

After that's done, I crank the music and enjoy the fifteen-minute drive.

Parking in front, I get out, running right into my dad.

"Daddy, what are you doing here?" I wrap him in a hug.

"Met him for lunch." He points to my surprise, at Tucker.

"I didn't know the two of you were having lunch together." I look at Tucker, trying to figure out if he was keeping this from me.

"It was last-minute. I had to go to the station, got my badge and gun back." He grins.

I throw myself into his arms, so excited for him.

"Anyway, I saw your dad walking down the sidewalk and thought he might like to have lunch."

"I wish I could join you two, but I'm just getting me and Kels lunch."

"It's cool, I think we'll be okay by ourselves." Dad gives me a look.

"Oh, I get it. This is a guy thing."

"Sorta."

While I'm excited the two of them are doing things without me and seem to be getting along, I'm a little bummed they don't want me to be a part of their lunch.

"See you at home?" Tucker gives me a hug, kissing me on the cheek.

"Yeah, see ya."

Tucker

"WHAT WERE the odds she was going to be here?" Pruitt asks as we take a booth in The Café.

"No fucking idea." I shake my head. "The one day I ask you to come have lunch with me, she shows up."

Our order is taken and dropped off quickly. They treat the Laurel Springs PD very well here and we thank them by spending most of our eating hours here.

"So," he asks as he positions his hamburger to take a bite, "what did you want to meet here to talk about?"

This is nerve-wracking, probably the absolute most nerve-wracking thing I've ever done, and I've done some shit in my life. "There aren't many things I follow the rules about," I start, putting my own burger down. "But this is one I feel like would be important not only for you, but for Karsyn too."

"I get the feeling this is an important conversation." He sets his food down.

"It is, and I know you probably feel like I'm moving too fast or this is being sprung upon you, but the fact is, I've loved your daughter for over a year. It took me a long time to come to grips with that love. I wasn't raised in the type of household that showed love easily, so I didn't really know what it was. I'm doing my best to be the type of man Karsyn deserves and one she can be proud of. I want more than anything for her to go to bed and wake up in the morning knowing she has a partner."

I stop for a second, trying to collect myself, trying to figure out if I'm even worthy of asking the question I want to of this man.

"Go on," he encourages me, and I don't realize until he encourages me that I actually need it.

"I want to ask for your blessing."

"My blessing?"

"To ask Karsyn to marry me. I'm not big on traditions or social norms like this, but I know she is."

He wipes under his eyes, and that tells me more than anything how touched he is.

"She is, and Karsyn means the world to us. I've seen how she's grown with you, how she's become more confident in herself. I have to admit, last year when you two broke up, I didn't know who you were. But I hated you. She lost that spark she has, she lost the sparkle, and I didn't know if she'd ever get it back."

"Hell, sir," I chuckle. "I didn't know if I'd ever get it back either. There's something about her, about the way she makes me feel. It's almost like I'm addicted, but I was too scared last year to give her that power over me."

"You're okay with it now?"

"I can't imagine my life without her."

Those are the truest words I've ever spoken.

"She's engrained herself so deeply into my life." I shrug. "My dog loves her more than he loves me. Which is dangerous, but I'm willing to allow it."

My heart is pounding as I wait to hear the answer.

"You promise you'll always take care of her?"

"With everything I have in me. As long as I can provide it, she will never want for anything. She'll be safe, she'll be loved, adored, and worshiped. Until I give my last breath, she will be the most important thing in my life."

He smiles. One that spreads across his face. "Then you have my blessing, Tucker. Welcome to our family."

We get up, hugging right there in the middle of The Café, and I don't think I've ever been so happy in my entire life.

EPILOGUE #1

Karsyn

The house is dark when I get home, but I'm not surprised. It's been a hot as hell day and we've decided to grill out tonight, as not to warm the house up too much. I picked up the sides on the way home.

"Tucker?" I yell as I approach the back porch.

"Yeah, we're back here." I can hear Major making his presence known.

Opening the gate, I see the two of them. My man standing in front of the grill, no shirt on, while Major sits next to him, probably waiting on some meat to be dropped. Climbing up onto the porch, I go over to them.

Tucker leans back, pursing his lips for a kiss. I oblige, resting against him slightly.

"Long day?"

"Super long. Just wanted to be here with the two of you. I hate when you're off and I have to work."

"You get so jealous," he teases me.

"Not because you're off work." I'm slightly offended. "But because I don't get to spend the time with you."

"Sure." He rolls his eyes good-naturedly. 'What did you get for sides?"

"Pasta salad and corn salsa. I picked up some tortilla chips too. I'll go change and get this stuff plated. Be right back."

He smacks my ass, causing me to look back at him. "You know it stings when I'm in scrubs."

"I know." He smirks. "I get a better sound from it."

It amazes me how easy our relationship has been in the months following the killing of Clarence. I'm not as tense as I used to be, and I feel like Tucker and I now know better how to be a couple. Life is just about perfect. I sigh as I change into comfortable clothes, but for a moment I look at my hand. The only thing that would make this completely perfect? A ring on my left hand.

"That was so good." I rub my stomach as we relax on the back deck.

"It really was," Tucker agrees, taking a drink off the bottle of beer he has in front of him. "I can't believe you want to play." He looks down at Major. "Let Karsyn throw for you, I'm tired."

Standing up, I coo at Major, who loves it. "Yeah, your daddy has been way too lazy today." I reach over for his ball and throw it.

"Don't make fun of me." Tucker, nudges me with his foot.

"Poor baby." I lean down when Major comes back with

the ball, and it's then, I see something around his neck. "What is this?"

Tucker quirks an eyebrow. "I don't know, maybe you should look at it."

Now I'm confused but intrigued. It's a little pouch, so I take it off his collar and open it up, turning it upside down. What tumbles out on the table makes me gasp. It's a ring box, along with a folded note.

With shaking hands, I unfold the note. I know Tucker, and he's not one for huge professions of anything, so the simple words mean the most.

I love you, Karsyn. I don't want to imagine my life without you. Marry me?

My hand goes in front of my lips to hold in the excited scream that threatens my throat. I look over and he's gotten out of his seat, now he's on his knee, waiting for me. He grabs the ring box, opening it for me to see it.

"Will you?"

All of my dreams are here on this porch. This man, this dog, this simple profession of love, and oh my God, this ring he holds in front of him.

"Did you ask my dad?"

"That day at The Café."

"Tucker! That was three months ago!"

He laughs. "I had to get my courage up."

"You don't ever need courage with me. Yes! Yes! Yes!"

He puts the ring on my finger, and then stands me up, taking me in his arms, spinning me around.

The ring I wanted so bad a few hours ago, is right where I imagined it would be, and my Enigma? He wasn't so hard to understand at all.

EPILOGUE #2

Tucker

Late August - A Year Later

"I normally wouldn't be running this meeting, but FEMA has requested that we be on call for the potentially devastating event in the Gulf this week." Mason looks out at all of us.

Today, he looks older than normal, almost like he believes all the reports that have been coming in. A Category Five Hurricane is barreling toward the Florida Panhandle and the Gulf Coast.

He pulls up a weather map. The storm looks even nastier than it has the past few times we've gotten an update, if that's even possible. With my left hand, I reach over, grabbing Karsyn's hand in mine. I smile slightly as I feel her do what she's done since she slipped the ring on my finger. She caresses it, playing with the symbol of our devotion to one another.

"Long-term impact has it making landfall at Pensacola.

As big as this hurricane is, I don't have to tell you what that means for the Alabama Gulf Coast, as well. We'll need the K-9's." He looks out at me. "Sorry to take you away from you new bride so quickly."

I shrug; it is what it is, and we both knew that when we signed up to be members of LSERT.

"The plan is for us to travel down a few days before estimated landfall and stay in Atmore. That puts us an hour away from Pensacola and we should be far enough inland not to be affected by the storm surge."

"We should be able to act quickly too," Cutter says from where he sits behind me.

"Exactly," Menace agrees. "Which is why we need a first wave. Overtime has been approved, this comes out of the Federal budget. What I need are two K-9's, ten police officers, and six EMT'S, along with a few nurses and whatever doctors we can spare. We'll caravan down and be ready to help where needed. We already have a semi full of rations we'll take with us, and once we get the all-clear, we'll get down to business. Potentially there could be a few waves of volunteers helping. As soon as the gulf counties get their situations squared away, they'll start relieving us."

The room is abuzz with what's going on. A week ago no one knew this system was even brewing out in the ocean. Now, we're roughly seventy-two hours before projected landfall.

"If I could have volunteers, please sign up on this sheet," Menace is shouting. "I'll personally get with your supervisors and verify we'll still have coverage here. You'll be notified tonight, and we'll convene at the LSPD in the morning. Thank you all for being willing to help."

I look at Cutter, who stands beside me. "You going?"

"Ain't got nothing else to do." He grins. Somehow I don't think his life is as easy-going as he wants everyone to think.

I shake my head at him. "See you in the morning."

There's no doubt Menace will send both of us, potentially all three of us, I look over at my wife.

"See ya. This looks like it's going to be one for the record books." He glances at the TV screen that's playing everywhere for all of us to see. "Who knows, maybe this is the event that's gonna change my life forever?"

I look at him. "You think so?"

"Something has to." He shrugs.

Famous last words.

Cutter's book releases June 2020!

CONNECT WITH LARAMIE

Patreon:
patreon.com/laramiebriscoe
Website:
www.laramiebriscoe.net
Facebook:
facebook.com/AuthorLaramieBriscoe
Twitter:
twitter.com/LaramieBriscoe
Pinterest:
pinterest.com/laramiebriscoe
Instagram:
instagram.com/laramie_briscoe
Mailing List:
http://sitel.ink/LBList
Email:
laramie@laramiebriscoe.com